ALMOST ONE

Born in 1951, Alex Hirst lives in South London. *Almost One* is his first published work.

ALEX HIRST

ALMOST ONE

GMP

First published June 1985 by GMP Publishers Ltd
P O Box 247, London N15 6RW, England.

Distributed in North America by
Alyson Publications Inc.,
40 Plympton Street, Boston, MA 02118, USA.

British Library Cataloguing in Publication Data

Hirst, Alex
Almost one.—(New gay writing)
I. Title II. Series
823'.914[F] PR6058.154/
ISBN 0–907040–69–1

Cover by Aubrey Walter
Typeset by M C Typeset, Chatham, Kent.
Printed and bound by Billing and Sons Ltd, Worcester.

for Mari Warner in Maputo
and Suzie García from Brooklyn

Poor Soul

Don't you perceive this dusk, rising from the teacups and the elegance, while silent ghosts observe our silhouettes? We are paralysed actors sitting in these garden seats, slowly vanishing into the night.

As though by chance, I see your mouth. As though by chance, I hear that unbearable voice of yours, calling from the airless Bronx. You are speaking of vulnerability and abandonment, the ashes and the excrements of desire. 'The hair is cropped in a final attempt to eroticise politics: thoughts come ready-packed as Leichner sticks, prepared for the worst: passion has become an integer of hatred, scratched in the chicken-houses and fuck-rooms where the spangles of desire spell parodies of "freedom" on walls designed for firing-squads . . .'

I know. It is 5 p.m., one Sunday in January. The river, at Greenwich, is red. Downstream, past the Isle of Dogs, it's already grey. Somewhere, someone is putting on his Nazi uniform, as though life really could just go on as normal.

Change. No change.

In a trice I was on Hampstead Heath. The people on the door had let me in because I was wearing denim and leather. I reached a clearing in the trees where the ephemera of illicit sex – mainly scraps of soiled Kleenex – were picked out for me like insects in the moonlight. Someone was walking towards me through this mess. I waited. Cropped hair, green bomber jacket, bleached jeans; a tall skinhead, about nineteen or twenty, and quite well-built, but not particularly butch. As he reached me, his eyes gave me a quick scan and, almost immediately, he was pushing my head down to his crotch. It was bulging, of course.

The scene changed to Rome. In a city park, a powerful Roman was being sucked off, leaning against a buttress of the Capitoline Hill. A real jawbreaker. The dismay when the Roman jerked his cock out of my mouth before orgasm, zipped it away (with difficulty), and left. I watched him walk down the steps and away towards the Tiber.

Quickly move to something else, anything really. Shall I fuck him, or he me? Fingers? Groupsex? Black? Horsedick? Hairy? Pisshouse? Turkish? Nazi-type? They weren't fantasies at all, just memories stored in the archive, tins of food for those moments of winter which invade most days. He and I were almost one at those times.

Auntie Janet had found an old diary of mine during one of her clear-outs. It was a blue plastic-bound book, made in the People's Republic. Naturally, she examined it, but she was defeated by my shorthand. Even I had trouble in fitting names to the initials, faces and places to the names: having unwittingly encoded a fragment of my present, I was now almost unable to decode my past. It was a diary which encompassed present, past and future – a skeleton record as well as a guide – but now all it would do was to symbolise that fragment of life inadequately. My latest form of journal-writing is different: there are no names, places or times, and no symbols with forgotten meanings; just a catalogue of feelings, each reduced to the immediate stimulus – drugs, sex, alcohol, etc. – with a mention for depression, when it 'began' and when it 'ended'. It's less comforting than the other type of diary, but less infuriating. There's no certainty in it, no unity or clarity of intent. It has its meanings and its areas of indistinction, perhaps emptiness or light, but it's not mystifying. It makes no attempts at spurious connections between myself and not-myself. (In any case, such attempts in the old diary are quite unintelligible.) Instead, it just reminds me of incidents and encounters which may as well be nameless, events which have interfered with my own spurious sense of connection with life.

If such events were not alienating, perhaps no-one would try and record them, perhaps no-one would need to kid themselves that they have a particular meaning or effect which somehow confers a reality upon existence. We should then escape our history and those distortions of its energy which are memories.

Siegfried, my uncle, maintains that he exists on the margin. He says he can't get away from it. I think my diary is the margin of a real journal. The elements of this margin are all synonyms of faith. The paralysed actors? It's difficult to know if they shine in their silence, or if they are just objects whose incandescence is an almost passive quality. Other than that, there are events, speculations, ironies. If I were more of a mystic, I might search for some symmetry in it all, some specific hope, an identity. But all I do is watch as it creeps relentlessly onto the page. Once there, it organises itself like a biochemical process, neither pretty nor repulsive. Then it waits. It even smokes a cigarette. It seems almost human.

In this landscape, which is varied if not familiar, there is a garden. Not a zen garden, which would be too formal, nor a garden of earthly delights, which would be overwhelming, but a small suburban garden with ornamental shrubs and a pond. I call it the *jardin d'hiver*, using the words more for their charm than for their significance. Perhaps it's in this garden that my body will be found.

The Winter Garden: Part I

Siegfried was sitting next to the electric fire, maudlin drunk. The overhead light was switched on. Forty watts of cheap-rate bleakness. He was addressing me as though speaking into a dictaphone:

'I'm not young and not old,' he said, 'neither poverty-stricken nor well-heeled; I don't have a career, or a structured commitment that I could call an anti-career . . . I can go on almost forever, defining myself in negatives. But how do I assert my *self* if none of the categories seem to fit? I haunt the margin, trying to get to know myself by a process of elimination, trying to recognise myself in my absence from definitions.' (Uncle Siegfried is waiting to be blinded by light on the road to Damascus.)

'Tell me about the margin, Uncle Siegfried,' I said, knowing that he was waiting for me to give him his cue.

'The margin,' he began, in his mock-turtle voice, 'is an area of ambiguity, of becoming and of ceasing to be. The pain lies in that pleasure, and vice versa: feelings as lacking in precise definition as the person who feels them. It's because I still have expectations of other people – I'm still willing to love them – that I find myself in this position.'

He paused to empty his glass and to fumble for a cigarette. He wasn't looking at me.

'The margin doesn't deal in commodities and respectability. It only acknowledges the process of becoming and the process of ceasing to be, and I can only hover, uncertainly, beside those processes. If I find it hard to define myself, I'm quite incapable of defining others or, if I do, it's in the knowledge that I'm betraying them. How can I say "This person is good. That person is evil."?'

I wasn't sure if he'd finished or if he required another prompt. I glanced up vaguely at the badly framed print of 'La Première Soirée', which Auntie Janet had cut out of *Woman's Journal* several years ago. She was fond of Renoir. My silence seemed to jar Siegfried into elaborating further.

'Being on the margin also means that usually I can't find words that seem to fit my environment. Other people often seem so sure of having or of not having something. They seem so sure of wanting things and so expert at avoiding the problem of being. I'm not even sure that I have a communicable language.'

Again there was a hiatus. I was beginning to lose his drift. He seemed to notice this.

'Of course I'm a consumer, too,' he said, rather paranoiacally, as though I'd accused him of concealing his own vices. 'But it doesn't really fool me: I can still tell the difference between my poems, which nobody likes, and my jokes, which everyone laughs at but which are actually just monkey-nuts to be hoarded or to pelt the passers-by with when I feel ignored. I don't mean that my poems are serious; they're just rare – sometimes so rare that they aren't made of words and images, but of blood. They don't have a language, just a life dying in my head.'

He suddenly smiled. 'A haemorrhage is an *escape* of blood from the arteries. A poem is an escape of love.'

One of Auntie Janet's major assets is her ability to sense the correct moment at which to interrupt Siegfried. Just as I was searching desperately for some sort of rejoinder to this imponderable remark of his, she entered, bearing a clotheshorse and a bowl of damp smalls. Siegfried and I watched in awe as she deftly assembled the structure in front of the fire, effectively screening it from us, and began to hang the clothes on the rails. 'I've had to bleach them,' she announced tartly. She didn't need to say what she really meant; we both knew from her tone of voice that we were to be ashamed of ourselves for some reason. We sat there in guilty silence as she went about her business. Her briskness was so overstated that we knew it was pointless to try and atone in words at that moment for whatever transgression we had committed.

Neither of us dared to complain that we couldn't feel the fire.

When she'd finished arranging the clothes, she was faced with the problem of finding some phrase or gesture which would humiliate us sufficiently for her to be able to leave the room in complete dignity. She made the admirable choice of the ashtray, which was overflowing. She lifted it, carefully and without a word, handling it as though it were an object she herself would never normally touch (she smokes about thirty a day), and delicately emptied it into a waste-bin. Then she replaced it, straightened out a slightly wrinkled vest on the top rail of the clothes-horse, surveyed the effects of her intrusion for a moment, and withdrew in silence to the kitchen. We were left alone again like two psychiatric patients who have inadvertently but incontestably aroused the wrath of their favourite nurse.

It isn't easy to deflect Siegfried from his course, though, and after a respectful but brief silence during which I continued my contemplation of the Renoir he began to speak again.

'Tragedy is precisely a consciousness of the experience of ambiguity – if you were *sure* that everything was shit, you wouldn't experience quite the same sense of devastation. People say that the choice between subject and object – me and them – is a false choice, but how do I know anything without making that initial separation? The margin where I exist is defined as not-being only because others define themselves and their environments so unequivocally (you might say *desperately*) as being, but it's a being which often fails to convince *me* of its authenticity . . .'

The underclothes were getting steamy, the smell of bleach gradually outdoing our cigarette-fumes.

'One thing I can be sure of, though, is that I and the margin I inhabit are in the late twentieth century. We have to sneak around the world as tensely as mice – it's neither the time nor the place for agonising about identity and personal truth. All we can do is steal our survival like mice; steal a quick fuck; steal a moment of tranquillity; steal someone else's sense of reality whenever possible. It's not a moral act: if we hurl ourselves at the windows of foodstores like ravenous vermin, who can blame us?

'The barricades are up again. If I stay in my margin now, I'll risk being shot at by both sides, but if I try to move to one side or the other, the margin moves with me. The barricades dissolve and rematerialise elsewhere. All enemies are ex-lovers.'

I felt like challenging this latter assertion, but thought better of it: Siegfried's eyes were fixed on the clothes-horse with terrible intensity. These sentences weren't being addressed to me, nor was his mind really focussed enough on my presence to make it worth my commenting on his words. I waited for him to continue. It was my duty.

'I fall in love,' he said eventually, 'with those who make no bones about being uncertain. Occasionally I meet someone who rejoices and despairs in lack of certainty.'

'Can gay people ever be certain . . ?' I ventured.

'Well,' he replied, though I suspected that it would be no reply at all, 'people know I fall for males, so they ask: "Are you gay?" It's another way of asking me if I'm certain, but of course I usually just say yes, even if I resent it. I say yes partly for political reasons, barricade-reasons, and partly because I used to think I was less uncertain than I am now about what "being gay" means. It's become a habit to say yes, like answering your name on the school register every morning. It saves trouble. I don't even really *mind* saying that I'm gay, although I'd prefer to say "nigger", which sounds much less ridiculous because it refers to a state of being rather than just to a state of mind. The fact is that I have to say *something* because people wouldn't be able to cope if, every time they asked an apparently straightforward question, I presented them with the story of my marginalisation. I don't think I'd be able to cope with it, either. But I don't enjoy having to fossilise myself with these quick definitions. It's almost a relief to be talking to you about the margin now, and about that cluster of not-belongings by which I nearly manage to discern myself, if only because I hardly ever mention it otherwise.'

This was rather a distortion, I felt. Uncle Siegfried seemed to me to spend a great deal of his time 'mentioning' the margin. And, of course, he hadn't answered my question at all, but I let it pass.

'So when I fall in love, or when someone falls in love with me, what happens?' He looked at me, as though it were I who had just asked him to explain the point.

'I think there are times,' he said, 'when I and others on the margin need a rest, but aren't quite ready for death. Falling in love isn't always very restful, but it's an opportunity for fantasy and illusion, a sort of rest from the desperation of everyday life. It's an opportunity for pretending that you're not really on the margin at all, that you do belong. It's possible to do that because lovers define themselves in terms of each other – a cruel illusion, but still an extraordinary process. They attempt the merger of subject and object and sometimes it can even appear to succeed. And if you both sustain that appearance it can seem to endure, at least until death. The most beautiful and perhaps the cruellest illusion, I think, is when lovers die together – each subsiding into the solitude of death without realising that they're alone. It's very convincing for us, the observers, too. But the illusions of the margin are built on uncertainties. They don't survive for long. The process of falling in love is almost inevitably followed by that of ceasing to be in love.' The girl of the Première Soirée gazed at whatever spectacle was unfolding on the stage. 'Orpheus in the Underworld', perhaps, or 'Madam Butterfly' . . .

'So where does all this leave me?' he inquired cheerfully, 'where does it get me to chart my position with epigrams? Neither behind, nor in front, nor any surer of my actual position. Should I despair? Would I benefit from therapy? Can I move? I am defeated by my own lack of faith, but saved by my reluctance to deny the possibility of faith . . . The margin is my cold comfort, shifting according to the conditions; but it's always there, everywhere, and everyone exists somewhere along it. Like invisible question marks hovering at the end of their own statements . . .' He got up and poured another drink.

'He and I were almost one at those times.' Give yourself a

start and you'll churn out a few associations; you'll cease to be alienated from literacy; in three years you'll begin to feel real and, if not, at least you'll feel like a neurotic Viennese lady with a special dream . . .

Am I one with the image of myself in a seedy bed-sit in Shepherd's Bush? A young bisexual was buggering me while we stared at ourselves – or at each other – in the wardrobe mirror. His pubic hairs banging against my pussy (his terminology, I'm sure). I got to fuck him first, but only as a preliminary, just something to get him going; he shat me out before I could come. As I left him, with his sperm oozing into the gusset of my jeans, I was a little nobody – my desire hadn't had the time to force an identity on me. The roundabout at the end of Holland Park Avenue, where Angelo had come into my mouth one summer's night, was just a roundabout.

Also a wardrobe mirror, this time in a Parisian hovel, some *chambre de bonne* littered with philosophy books. He was naked; I wore his leather jacket, nothing else. I inserted a candle into him after pretending to violate him with my dick. We jerked off, staring at the mirror. I think he was a scat-queen.

I dream of murder, but I only remember sex. I was standing against the wall of the cruisiest part of the Catacombs, young and alone. Various older men were interested. I suppose they imagined how willingly I would yield, how smooth, firm and tight I would be. A predator touched my crotch and I moved back, pressing myself against the wall. My stomach was flattened. He put his hand on it. 'You'll be old yourself one day,' he said nastily. 'You'll get a belly like mine.' I was meant to ensure against the inevitable experience of being rejected for my age in the future by overcoming my distaste for this man and permitting him to use my body for a while. He didn't understand that it wasn't his age which bothered me, nor even particularly his beer-gut.

The memories are more commonly of sexual events rather than sexual feelings. That's why the new diary is such a departure for me. But there's still quite an overlap of memory and emotional record: I haven't been able to forget the one about the ladies' lavatory at Heaven. An American dream with moustache and no foreskin, just like in the magazines. As I was fucking him, a head appeared over the wall, and then a hand, offering amyl nitrite. The voyeur was wearing a leather cap. I could tell that he was jerking off as he watched us. Afterwards, the dream, who had seen none of this (he'd been too busy watching his own dick and hitting himself blind with poppers) turned to me – his wet lips were now rather dry – and smiled: 'But *I* was gonna fuck *you*!' Do people really talk like that?

Some people claim to fantasise or reminisce about feelings during their jerk-offs. Is that being less or more alienated than me? Which of us is making the most of our selective autobiographies? It's a certain fastidiousness, no doubt, on either side, which provokes this fragmentation.

There was a boy in the covered market in Bradford, sitting opposite me in a greasy pie-and-peas caff. He was blond and tough; ice-blue jeans, fashionable then, and an enormous dick going halfway down his leg. A classic male image of the deviant demigod. He invited me by touching the bulge of his cock. We had a quick one, with kisses (showing his true colours – tough kids fuck but never kiss), in a back alley somewhere. Nameless; an unidentified location; it was sometime in the afternoon, one Saturday, years ago.

It's impossible to invoke jerk-off memories of lovers. The minute feelings or memories of feelings threaten to appear, the search-button looks for another image. Sadness and masturbation don't mix. Sadness is too remote and cerebral, like a mother waving goodbye. Forget your lover, forget your mother, at least until you've come. (Who can play with his dick in front of the altar without its becoming just an exercise in self-pollution?) Think of selfness and utter otherness instead: the story of the blues party in Clapham where some honky got fucked by six men. Much better, actually, was that hard-hat on the Heath who was fucking an almost insensible queen. I touched the dick while it was stuffed up the queen's arse. A black boy who was standing next to me had a feel, too. Then he pulled his pants down and pressed back against my cock. His arse was incredibly tight – I couldn't get it in, but I liked the gesture. Complete, irrational trust between strangers. It makes me come.

The more alienated the memory of the event, the closer I am to (him) while I'm remembering it: no need to think of the other's thoughts and feelings, which, in any case, are rarely expressed – not memorably, that is.

With lovers, it's different. Knowing something about them means tears, warmth, even dreams. Remembering it is what comes between us. I recall those things when I'm not jerking off. It's another kind of memory, an ambiguous communion with history which is almost as difficult to deal with as memories of one's family. With objectification, however, you know more or less where you are.

The new diary lists sex-acts. Some of them are mentioned as *N/A sex* (non-alienated), some as *sex,* others as *alienated.* One entry is *unsex*. 'What do you mean by "non-alienated"?' someone asked. A question lacking in taste, I thought.

This bit is a collection of my Rubáiyát, a nod to the nomadic principle, and one in the eye for those cultural types with their ordered furrows and their fucking ploughs.

A nude beach near Rome: two young Italian bike-boys sprawled over each other, their bikes flung down in the sand. It was late in the afternoon as we walked past; our shadows fell across them for a moment and the droplets of sweat or sea-water on their bodies, glinting in the light, seemed to vanish. They were like cats. Let's keep this image, not for its sexiness, but because it's so romantic.

Same beach, a different afternoon. In the scrubland behind the dunes, wandering around naked, and feeling vulnerable. Occasional glimpses of boys and men, either already engaged in sexual activity, or still alone, casual and graceful. I lay down on my stomach in the hot sand. I must have drifted off into sleep. I was awakened by a soft tickling feeling between my legs. I turned my head, and the man quickly withdrew his hand from my butt. He was a thickset Roman, about thirty, with moustache, chest-hair and a hard cock in his other hand. We kissed, jerked off, parted.

Cut to a park. A young proletarian puts my hand on his crotch. 'Suck me. I won't come in your mouth.' He didn't keep his promise, but as though to compensate, he stayed to jerk me off (even casual sex can be generous). I watched him piss against a tree afterwards. His friends would never have guessed that he'd just done a favour for some little cocksucker in the bushes.

A dank apartment in Milan. A Neapolitan rent-boy admires my dick. Generosity again, and all he wants is two thousand lire. He says he'll bring me a girl tomorrow and we'll both have a good time. It's his way of not being queer. I told him I was broke, and he left with a sandwich instead of the money.

Or the station at Naples, full of rent-boys. I looked great that summer, my piss was a heavy stream, very male, even my dick was suntanned. He was showing me his cock and smiling – a real hunk. But I was already late, no time to even touch him. I've always regretted it. His smile was almost enough, but not quite.

Once, in Rotterdam, a boy fucked me using shaving soap. I gave him my favourite self-portrait: a fine boy with clear, blue eyes, smiling. I can be generous, too.

Still in Rotterdam, a bike-boy with a very attractive cock forced it up my arse at a time when I wasn't used to accommodating much more than a tentative finger. I think he felt KY was too prissy. After four days I had to leave. Even that kind of brutality can be too much. I spent that night in a paedophile's trailer in Amsterdam, watching him play with two straight German boys, who were willing to put up with it for the sake of somewhere to sleep. They pretended not to look at each other's hard-ons.

On a train, outside Amiens or somewhere, the Venezuelan sitting opposite me touched my knee with his knee. I remember his arse as he bent over the lavabo. Who cared what the people queuing up outside must have thought?

A Libyan from what used to be the embassy took me to a flat in Earl's Court and informed me that 17% of his countrymen had sex with other men. He didn't mind shoving his cock up my arse, but he couldn't cope with touching my dick. Did we kiss? Probably. Kissing isn't as bad as touching someone's dick.

I was jerking off in the front of a lorry as we entered Lyons. Nobody but the driver could see. He loved it.

Reggie was one of the best. He had canerows and a dancer's body, though he was really a soul-singer. When he discovered that his dad was a faggot, he went directly to Fire Island and came out. His wife divorced him.

As we were about to leave a nightclub in Paris, he looked around at the other black clients, and in his New Jersey purr, he declared: 'Alex, I am the *finest* nigger in this place.' He knew it was true. He used to make me come without even having to touch my dick. Just the pressure against my prostate and the feel of his tongue in my mouth were enough. It was the kind of orgasm that starts in your hands and feet and makes you feel faint.

Reggie wasn't a lover; our backgrounds were really too diverse.

This is a walk, but not in the Paradise Garden. It's a hundred paces or so, past the flowers, under the light, watching the little murders, living honourably enough, discovering neither too much nor too little. The generosity of those living bodies makes me feel real. Their arms catch me as I fall, even though they don't have to. They smile, even when it's cold and wet. They tell jokes (what could be more respectful?). A hundred paces gives you just enough to transform desolation into a sign of devotion. So what if it may only be a temporary sign?

Part II

Alex used memories even after he met Andy, though I think he preferred memories of Andy himself for jerking off. (At least until they split – after that, he couldn't jerk off much for weeks, and certainly not with memories of Andy; and sex itself was totally out of the question.) When they . . . had sex during the last weeks of being together, he seemed to need memories less and less. Andy's body made him forget – his hair, often cropped and bleached or tinted, his chest, already furry, his belly, always warm; the rather unhappy eyes, nervous and over-modest, the caresses, the moist nuzzling of his lips; his breath, his sweat, the silence. It sounds almost grotesque to mention these things now, but perhaps only because of the context. And perhaps that immediacy of experience, which in the end is incommunicable and therefore a mystery, is the closest Alex got to some part of himself after all. Andy's soul is all that anyone needs to see. The rest is metaphor.

What *is* the context of these remarks, anyway?

Categories would only trick you, like footnotes to a poem. Why not look through a few snapshots, instead? Images structured only by ingenuousness and the desire to please the part of you which is still unattached to the electronic eye: Paris, May 1968; Huddersfield, June 1981; Venice, February 1982 (the unlosable spirit at the scene of lost causes). Do you recognise the one of me with the long hair and the flares; the one with blue skinhead hair and the pendant earring; the one in the vinyl mini-skirt and the blond wig; the army greens and mascara; the Alhambra, Christmas 1977, with my arm around a woman? The bleached quiff and disco rag-bag look is actually a perverse home-movie. Oh God, he's allowing me to TOUCH HIS DICK!

Reality disintegrates with these memories. They interrupt the apparent continuum of life, reminding me of my alter 'egos', not letting me get away with thinking that, now, as a result of those past images, I'm somehow whole. They insist on telling me what a fragment I always am, and how innumerable the fragments are that huddle uneasily together under the protection of my name.

'Come inside me,' said Pietro in Italian. Then he asked me if I understood what he meant.

'Yes,' I replied.

We're all cheap sometimes, let's face it. Even Auntie Janet is occasionally cheap. But for most of the time I think she has quite a lot of class, considering her circumstances.

Janet isn't Uncle Siegfried's wife. She's unmarried and getting on in years. Alex doesn't hate her. He doesn't resent her presence in his life; on the contrary, he sometimes thinks he'd do well to spend more time with her than he actually does. After all, she's taught him a lot, for instance everything he knows about food-snobbery: 'Basmati, NOT Uncle Ben's'. She's also taught him how to wash up properly afterwards.

Of course, Siegfried finds her a bit of an embarrassment, especially the bitching and gossiping, the slightly risqué jokes, the interminable interest in the minute details of other people's existence – Janet's fear of death is really a fear of missing an instalment of trivial scandal, a fear of not being able to receive the news that so-and-so actually used *tinned* kidney beans to prepare what was claimed to be an authentic Caribbean delicacy. Even worse is that thought that death may prevent her from reporting such news as was received to her carefully selected circle of lady-friends (none of whom is actually *malicious*, but they're all rather frightening connoisseurs of human folly).

It's difficult, then, (you can imagine) for me to contemplate the act of jerking off in virtually the same breath as I mention my aunt. But I don't feel that so central a conflict should be avoided. Jerking off, as I'm sure most teenagers realise by now, used to be defined in dictionaries as 'self-abuse', as though the compilers and their moral tutors had actually understood the complex spiritual process which occurs during the act; had understood that jerking off is a dangerous, if temporary, assault on the 'self', which can otherwise often manage to preserve a semblance of integrity. In the privacy of a bedroom, a lavatory or a dark alley, the person jerking off surrenders to the disintegration of that makeshift self which is so precious to moralists, healers and right-wing theorists. It has to be a private act, or if performed in public, then only with people who are already, though perhaps not consciously, moving beyond good and evil: in the concentration camp hut, in a piss-house, in the bushes on the Heath, in a doss-house for vagrants, or behind the cookhouse in the second form at school. Even then, there are degrees of publicity. Jerking off in front of a video camera is, unfortunately, more a question of confidence than of exposed ecstasy: it's about as genuine as the prayers of our gibbering Pope.

The usual jerk-off privacy allows the tensions of the social self to disperse; the masks disappear, not to reveal a 'real self' beneath, but a multiplicity of memories, desires and moral scars. An almost random selection of the fragments of life assert themselves temporarily, and for once are acknowledged, tolerated, even enjoyed. Solemnity and hysteria gasp out their communion in monosyllabic interjections which aren't even funny. The solitude which you find so difficult to cope with at other times – seeking the company of others is a way of trying to feel whole – becomes a pleasure, even a prerequisite of further solitary pleasure. That arc of useless spunk is your vengeance, a god to be wiped up and thrown away a million times, so often in fact that death, though indisputably unique, seems almost restrained in comparison. *Pulling your self together* after orgasm isn't a dead metaphor at all.

Accepting and enjoying this solitude after Andy left would have contradicted what I wanted to feel then: a sense of *loss*, that paradox by which the desperate validate the sense of having been together. Being in love required us both to try and be whole in the other's eyes; it forces us to construct wholeness out of images of each other. Eventually he looked elsewhere, while I, still wanting him, suppressed my fragmentation in favour of an illusory whole which I still wanted him to love.

Non-monogamists are such a threat because those happily-married-ever-after types can't perpetuate their dream of wholeness and togetherness in an atmosphere of uncertainty. Monogamy must be for ever; it must have a meaning . . . it's dangerous to realise that meanings change, and that change, in itself, may be enough of a meaning. It's dangerous to realise that there's no eternity.

Boys jerk off. Auntie Janet washes the sheets without a murmur.

An American in Paris shared some drugs with me, before we went to bed. He had Arctic eyes and a tropical dick. The drugs suppressed erection for a while, leaving time to contact each other by the oral-anal route (we were too crazed to worry about hepatitis, too irresponsible to deny ourselves the thrill of being bestial). I got a hard-on first and fucked him, but he was the one who finally spurted into my gut. It was because I was younger than him.

An American in London. We did it in the pre-War German Embassy. He was older, too, but he had the decency to warn me: 'If I start fucking you, you'll never get me out.' I fucked him first, and chose not to wonder whether he was really very devious – playing butch for me just so that I'd fuck him better.

In South London a boy in motor-mechanic overalls showed me his dick at the urinal. It was like having your hair washed by someone beautiful whose crotch is brushing against your shoulder: my whole body was sensitised. I was shaking.

Bondage memories don't crop up very often, though perhaps we should all have at least one, something to make us feel safe and unsafe like a three-day growth of beard on the face of any young queer. There's an off-beat one where Alex was trussed up in front of a mirror. The excitement was meant to be increased, I think, by the feeling of physical restraint, and to be visibly confirmed by the reflected image. It wasn't, but the sight of himself - blond quiff, lightly tanned skin between the straps of leather - was actually touching. The other person murmured, 'You have such a lovely face.'

Tenderness is sometimes irrepressible.

There was a glory-hole between two lock-up cubicles in a Berlin piss-house, ideal for doing something wicked. We could observe each other through it without having to make much of an effort. He was moving his bowels rather than loitering, but, perhaps because he was Turkish, he wasn't averse to unconventional orgasm. His cock appeared through the hole. I thought how easy it would be to damage it. On this occasion, I acquiesced to his power, however, and acquired a memory. Another person might have smashed the end of his dick in, but I jerked him off and watched his sperm slither down the tiles.

Those Berlin-fools will tell you all sorts of stories: their meat-hook trip through the lost city. The place is no more than a memory for me, however *chic* and questionable. But it all happened some years ago, before Christopher Isherwood had repenetrated the market, and when David Bowie was still in a space-suit. Siegfried and I went there together, expecting miracles. We couldn't afford couchettes, so we spent the night in the Soviet-style dining car, drinking. We'd been chattering about this and that for some hours before the heaviness started. I had made some harmless remark about the 'special status' of Berlin when he suddenly roared:

'*Every* city is a myth. *Every* city is an approximation of realities camouflaging even more –'

I looked at him mildly, almost indulgently.

'You can dismiss me as an eccentric if you like,' he snorted, 'but just remember that I feel the inadequacy of my words even more poignantly than you.'

Apparently undeterred, he took another swig of pilsner and carried on as though he had not just interrupted himself:

'When I say "realities", what I mean is a multiplicity of

meanings, a sexuality which overlaps, opposes, and engenders itself in endless cycles. Each meaning vies with the others in obscuring perception of the whole. The whole is barely sensed, except in the most banal geographical way. An understanding of the whole would be more than the collective intellect of entire populations could apprehend. It remains as fluctuating as they do, and reflects in this aspect one of their most disturbing attributes: it has the power of invisibility.'

My responsibility as Siegfried's wicket-keeper was to throw back his no-balls.

'How do you mean?' I asked.

What I was really interested in was whether the list I'd copied from the Spartacus Guide was still up-to-date.

'I mean that it recedes behind the surface of its own creation, like a god. It becomes only partially accessible, through the medium of lesser gods or priests who are also constantly threatening to vanish and leave only memories or imagined visions. The city has the quality of a myth because, like the world, it's still beyond human control.'

Even if my uncle didn't realise it, I knew that we were approaching the frontier between East and West, an experience which has its relationship with Death. It seemed appropriate that Siegfried should be so desperate to speak that he didn't even notice that we were soon to be obliged to participate in the very specific myth – the ritual crossing of the Iron Curtain – on which the northern hemisphere manages to sustain itself.

'The city is a temple still under construction,' he said, charmingly oblivious to the floodlights down the track. 'There's been an almost total loss of consciousness concerning the architecture of it: all the buildings are symbols. But it wouldn't be enough to discover the "original" meaning of these symbols. It has to pass through your existence – a transformation of your being within the city and of the city within you. It's like an alchemical process – a confrontation with ambiguity from which you have to distil new images. Archaeology and iconoclasm –' The train suddenly jolted and stopped. That shut him up. It was rather a relief for me – not that I was bored, but I was beginning to get a feeling of vague dismay to be reminded yet again that my uncle's passions were so cerebral. Perhaps he made me feel guilty. The border guards came through to scrutinise us and keep us busy while the engine was changed. After that Siegfried dozed off for the rest of the journey. A few hours later, we were in 'Berlin', homeless, unemployed, and with £50 between us.

My real reason for going there was the memory of Achim, a morgue-attendant in that city, dark and moustached, in leather, whom I'd watched pissing into the gardens of a square in South Kensington before I took him home for sex. Achim had thrown me around the room, fantasised me as a Jew, forced me to cocksuck, obliged me to be fucked in dog-position; however, he'd also permitted me to poke my tongue intimately between his thighs, and while he was sleeping, I'd held his soft, but still slightly swollen dick while jerking myself off. (Naturally, he hadn't bothered about whether I came or not during the act, so I was left to deal with that myself while he pulled the quilt around himself and greedily edged me out of the bed.)

Of course, I never found him in Berlin. Probably a mercy that I didn't. And if I had? Perhaps it wouldn't have been surprising to find him settled down, pottering around the garden in jumble-sale clothes, while his lesbian companion was taking the dogs out over the fields. And elsewhere, to find the unfortunate armies of two opposing worlds giving a salute to the dusk.

What I did find in the Walled City, apart from fifteen degrees of frost and *four* armies of occupation, was a *tableau vivant* of the 'Inferno': it was infested with some of the most devastating sodomites north of the Alps, who reflected the post-War brutality of their environment in a parody of pre-War 'decadence' and guilt-ridden undenazified sex. Some people are still into that sort of thing.

At the time I wasn't inclined to let my ideas get in the way of my sexual practices. I just joined in the all-night frenzy and spent the days visiting those Weimar Republic urinals where bolder tourists can touch the exhibits with their icy fingers.

The GI's certainly lived up to Auntie Janet's cautionary

wartime tales, although the nylons and cigarettes had been replaced by heavier drugs. American soldiers were still fucking each other in Vietnam when Siegfried and I boarded the train for Paris.

Some memories are more lyrical than others.

It was spring. The new blossoms of the year were tumbling into brief splendour, measuring specific gravities and portions of blancmange – as though anybody cared. I did. In a urinal I discovered the first symptoms of a dose of time and space disease, an acquired immune deficiency. I prepared for the crisis: just in case I had to go to hospital, I made sure I groomed my morphine-scented belly-hairs and put on clean fetish-wear. But the preparation was largely a question of spiritual dispersal.

Then I entered the night, the one they keep locked out behind the doors of neighbouring houses (as though doors made any difference). I contemplated death as I left – a piece of meat (my brother, my sister, who knows?) was hanging conveniently in the pantry. Having penetrated the first shadows (the rays of an electric lamp still trespassed vaguely on the frontier), I encountered a man. His metal legs; his sofa guarded by elephants on golden pedestals; his abnormally-dilated pupils. He is Ivan.

He smiled at me, while his mouth whirred with the entire telephone exchange expressed in whispers on his lips.

It seemed that the secondary stage of this illness involved a session of mutual masturbation. 'No kidding!' is the cry. 'We buy anything. Our prices are ridiculous.'

With my pants round my ankles, I sprawled in front of the fire. In my wishing-well, I wanted his mind to be as V-shaped and lovely as his back. My hands were exploring his spleen.

It turned out that there was no terminal stage. Nothing to correspond to my presages or to justify my preparations: just 30p for my bus fare home, and the promise of another spring next year.

Meanwhile, my hypochondria was beginning to sink its teeth into the buttocks of summer – frangipane on Hampstead Heath. If you take the trouble to look for it.

Hampstead Heath or Monaco, where the gypsies dance on tables. I want to go to Monaco, quick-quick, quick-quick-slow, wrapped up in Russian sables.

If you still want to be friends and you're thinking that my arse is shrunken and withered because your dick hasn't prised its way in there for while, I think you'd better stop fooling yourself that you're such a big boy. If you still want to be friends, you'd better kiss my leather jock-strap or lie in the bath while I try to squeeze a few drops of piss out onto your belly, or you'd better shove your finger up your own tight arse, but purely for my benefit. As it is, I can't remember you at all. That's how strong *I* am. I can't remember you or my real-feeling self as you hammered away at my rectum. It's a shame that you power-stricken men turn out to be ponces in the end. You couldn't even be bothered to fuck me, or if you could, it seems to have slipped my mind. I can remember to buy Harpic with less effort than it takes to recall the shape of your dick. If I'm being a bit venomous now it must be because of the enema – that sick little protein-enema of yours which you hoped would rape me when I was screaming at you for sex. All you wanted was for me to shut up and die, you wanted the final shudder of my flesh to give you an orgasm. What you haven't realised yet - will you ever? - is that friends respect each other. Your silent fear is just depressing.

A mesembryanthemum, a clump of night-scented stock. I was peeping through a hole in the door to see if there was any trade at the urinals. This piss-house was reasonable, like many provincial public lavatories: Virgilio, just back from New York and infested with God knows what ghastly disease, had shown me the size of his cock in there (before taking me home for a fuck which was out of the question: even *my* arsehole has limits). After a while, a dark Sicilian entered and flashed his semi-hard-on nonchalantly. Later, parked in a car in the woods, this Luigi sucked me off. Why do people do these things? It wasn't until he took me home a few days later - his wife was at work; his daughter safe at kindergarten – that he fucked me in the bathroom. At my flat, later still, he let me investigate his man's sweet little arse. Almost hysterically he was assuring me that this type of thing was quite normal in Sicily. All the boys did it, not like in Milan. And did I know any very *young* boys who would like to meet him? At which point, my landlady began hammering on the door (how many Italian landladies can be content with a knock?), bringing the plumber. Luigi looked sick; he disengaged his arse from my finger, snatched up his clothes and flew into the bathroom. Afterwards I heard him sneaking down the back stairs. His body was almost perfect.

Part III

What do lovers take when they leave? It all becomes so calm and remote, but so utterly barbaric: their records, a coffee-pot, some sheets . . . Andy took whatever it was that left the waiting-space. Some of my confidence(s), I think. Who can judge whether he put that to good use?

The space was left for me to tackle. Space and time. Several months at least, though what do measurements matter? Seconds or years, it's all eternal until it ends. So with the space. Even the tiniest vacant lot is an incubus, a pain desperately waiting to be relieved, an emptiness begging to be filled, but filled only by boils. The time begs to pass, but lingers like immortality. Endlessness, which is only really appreciated at points such as these, is a more distressing idea than finitude. At points such as these, when endlessness is no longer just an idea, there are no more words.

And precisely at this point, when memory could have been so . . . useful, it too became impossible. The apparently useful; the apparently gratuitous: both hover above your sense of loss, indistinguishable, unattainable, awaiting recognition . . . a knife? So what? Better to collapse on the floor with a photograph of a knife and several photographs of blood, and thus to float between becoming and ceasing to be without asking 'why?'.

I goosed a little despair to kill the time of day. The auctioneer raised the dead in the uneasy absence of a cut-price mortuary or even a sapphire-escape. I lay in (his) arms in privacy, my mind creeping about the room, hand over hand along the iron pole. I avoided all the walls, carefully and laboriously, as though to touch them were to die (yes, one is still furious enough to stay alive).

From the poignant seclusion afforded on occasion by another's embrace, I could observe the crawling larvae which infested (our) room so overwhelmingly, and yet which under less auspicious circumstances were not at all apparent. Nameless obscenities struggled from their nests; my mind was filled with boring little flowers. Worlds refused to exist. Within that void (his) caresses were strangled. They became dreams, confused with the memories of lovers' eyes. The fluids of fleshless nights stained the intimacy of sleep and wakefulness. I found powdered sperm on the threadbare sheets. (Your) mouth – that red mouth belonging only to the world – was still singing for joy, still loving to be human. Its insolent lips hadn't yet learned to scream. (Screaming was a crisis among those dislocated days – the pain fascinated, but never enlightened.) This room of (ours) was a palace of unintelligible fears, where words were forgotten. It was here that (our) half-decayed desires haggled for a moment's peace with the ephemera of love. (You) committed (your) cream to my memory. (Your) drawl was struggling for worlds. (Our) love was a long sentence, mispronounced by chance, and consumed by its own deceptions in the tender hours, when (we) groped for dawn and (our) eyes encountered desolation in the kisses that collapsed into indifference.

But hearts and promises make the day – break – away. And love is a wilder mystery, beyond the most savagely indifferent despair. You wept too.

In time I met a skinhead, the type of person who by adopting their image is pleading with his oppressors to show him some affection. He wore a cockring and had a foot-fetish. His body wasn't lithe and muscular and hypersensitive. He didn't have a vigorous growth of hair under his arms or showing just above the waistband of his 501's. His lips didn't defy description; nor did his eyes leave me speechless. He didn't even give me the willies. He just spent hours licking my feet and legs. But what I liked about him was he was playing with himself the whole time.

(This book is not for use as an examination text.)

Two Caribbeans on the Heath: one older than me; one

younger. I wanted to fuck the older one, but he didn't dare: his arse was his problem, not mine, but it pissed me off. We went to North Tottenham somewhere – a suburb where the violence of the petit-bourgeois broods in the terraced houses beneath cane-and-glass dining tables like the viciousness of a weasel. The daddy watched while I fucked the boy. He was playing with the biggest horsedick I'd ever seen, but he says, 'Go easy. He's never had anyone but me.' I took his advice, even though I felt he was being a little over-cautious, and then watched in awe and fascination as we changed over: all that dick, sliding in so easily. The boy, perhaps he was a fakir, didn't even wince.

Back in the park in Rome: it's a tiered earthwork, rising up the Hill. The Theatre of Marcellus, discreetly illuminated, flanks the right. To the left, in semi-darkness, is the Forum. There is a definite sense of grandeur here, in the spectacular gloom. What could be more appropriate for a surrender to desire than in the shadow of the ruins of Imperial power? The caged she-wolf is sleeping; the wild cats – 'They do not let themselves be touched' – are hunting in the undergrowth with even more stealth and determination than the human males on the footpaths. The air is still so warm that the whole place is in a state of semi-erection: behind the flies of immaculately faded jeans, within the snugness of expensive cotton slips, the coils of Southern European sexuality reveal the threat of their languid pulse. Siegfried, however, never tiring of a tourism which, though off-beat, often failed to inspire me, had dragged me off to the Railway Station.

I discovered that it wasn't as tedious as I'd imagined. The station exists, materially, on a number of levels. The neo-Fascist superstructure provides columns against which the sub-proletariat can lean casually and with style, whether the style is effete and classic-elegant or butch and scruffy. It also provides timetables with a suitable framework: trains to Belgrade, Copenhagen and Palermo, expressed as casually on the posters as the vicious murmurs on the lips of the boys who lean against them.

Beneath, in the 'daytime hotel', there are baths and classy

lavatories for the weary bourgeoisie down from Milan. But there are too many busybodies here for there to be much chance of action. In the deepest layer is the Metropolitan Railway, authentically Fascist, if you like that sort of thing, providing an opportunity and a monumental environment for the presence of squalid toilets, much policed, but nevertheless constantly in use by some of the hottest young men in Rome. Some are just renting; others wouldn't say no to the offer of a few thousand lire, but they'll do it without if they like the look of you. One of them liked Alex enough to accept a gush of his English sperm.

A station, then, which among other things left Siegfried bemused but feeling poetic, and would bequeath Alex with a few memories to invoke when thinking 'What next?'

Sex in Rome often seemed to occur as though I were in a mild delirium. Perhaps because I was so remote from any milieu or subculture which may have existed; perhaps because it was so often street sex, back-alley sex, or the sex that happens behind low walls or in clumps of bushes, like pissing.

A Sardinian boy and I were going home together when we met a Bergamasque, a young blond with brown skin and azure eyes. It was on the bus. I spent the night with them in a kind of trance. Regret when the boy from Bergamo came just before I could fuck him; pleasure when the Sard delicately pushed his sex into me. It happened in a bed still warm from the body of the woman who usually slept there. Outside on the balcony, Jayne was crouching in the heat, having another cigarette. A woman-guest was sleeping fitfully on the cool marble in another room, being bitten by mosquitoes. I was aware, for once, of breaking taboos.

But Siegfried was beginning to feel old that summer: 'I'm not even thirty yet,' he told me one evening, as we were walking back home from some hideous *borgata*. 'Lucky me! Still time to jabber "Still time!" while I lose my footing on God's slime in the vaults of Nietzsche's lavatory. Still time to fall in love, and then crawl back out to dry on the balcony of death. But the creature I carry on my neck is beginning to bulge and grunt in his sack. Growing year by year. How many more two-faced minutes before I hear the clanging of the oven-door?'

'Shall we go back to London, then?'

'Why not?' he murmured in his peevish way. 'The philosophy of old men is even clammier than their feet. And I expect your Auntie Janet will be pleased to have us back.'

We were silent until we reached the outskirts of Monte Sacro.

'No scampering hare,' he said, 'only the bowels of an ex-hare, moving irregularly. No prize-money now; only the joke-shop – the fun-house of our privacy. Give me some hard drugs: my eyes need artificial light.'

We left on the next available flight.

When we got to bed, Alan started to fuck me, boyishly (that means that he didn't do it dishonestly), then withdrew. He put two fingers in my arse. 'I'm not going to fuck you,' he said, as though I'd asked him to; 'I'd rather touch you up.' He jerked off, excited, I suppose, by the image of touching my most intimate place, my most forbidden and vulnerable zone. I jerked off too, excited at having permitted him this pleasure.

At such times, gods are obsolete unless they kiss.

With Andy I was harsh: lovers are so far from one's dreams. It was only afterwards, in that more remote but quite serene region where sex is replaced by mutual respect that I could be really as indulgent towards him as I wanted to be, or could really show him the tenderness I felt. (That tenderness I felt once when I got home from work to find him hiding his shaved head under the bed-clothes as though it made him invisible, but I pretended not to be moved and barely even smiled.) Respect, fear, the suppression of words, sentimentality – the Mafia or even some cheap South Bronx street-gang would be proud of me . . .

In dark places, just before or after near-anonymous sex, I can accept almost anything, listen to their rubbish smilingly, gloss over the more grotesque aspects of their disingenuous behaviour, tell them whatever they want to hear. They have nothing to live up to, and I have nothing to lose. In fact, I lose myself every time, though not arbitrarily. Whoever my 'partner' happens to be, he elicits a response from me which I can't refuse. I'm like an unpaid prostitute, trying to work out which fantasy my client requires, somehow unable to feel confident that, this time, I'm the client. It's because I want them to desire me more than I desire them; I want to be able to bestow unpaid-for favours; to avoid the terror of discovering that my desire exceeds theirs, no matter how sublime the curve of their buttocks. That's what is so bitter in the after-taste: both parties accept the unspoken contract which states that each shall take what he can get away with, each shall give only what he has to spare, neither will reveal any feeling, only a brute hunger which must be appeased immediately. Though both may dream, in secret horror, of love. Being harsh with a lover is part of the process of tempting (him) to stop loving you – that desperate, death-inspired need to have it confirmed that all love is ephemeral: *when* will it end? It's like saying 'Why not stop now? You know you will eventually', but to which you still want the impossible answer 'Never!' This is the religious aspect of being in love.

Being harsh is a way of fighting that religiosity, while paradoxically still yearning for it. Your harshness obliges (him) to seek within (himself), not in you – though perhaps it's more often a matter of encouraging (him) to look to someone else, and prevents (him) from saying what you most want to hear. It's a reminder, both comforting and painful, that you survived without (him) before . . . but after the harshness, when both of us move into unwilling self-sufficiency, love emerges momentarily free from clingings and resentments to celebrate the uncertain pleasure of finding each other's existence, each other's body, close together in the night. Hollywood has done nothing but reinforce religious panic.

What do lovers take with them when they leave?

I boiled your beef; you stewed my prunes. I scraped your

potatoes; you basted my joint. I mashed your tea; you tossed my pancake. I baked your beans; you roasted my chestnuts. I glazed your pears; you jellied my eels. I jugged your hare; you peeled my shrimps. I opened your tin; you poached my eggs. I stuffed your marrow; you kneaded my dough. And when I cooked your goose, you whipped my cream and didn't even leave a tip!

Love foams and steals away, like a jackal after the frolics of an evening meal shared with a palpitating friend (his heart trembled for me). Our carcasses grow mushrooms in the shadow of orgasm. Solitude is more than a creeping grief, more of a disease breaking and entering than just another feeling to memorise for old age. I am food for the starving millions (the miracle of the loaves and fishes, the mystery of the Transubstantiation), but I crawl from your fork to hide and fester in the cracks of a dirty floor while you frogmarch a mirage through your private graveyard, hoping to find happiness in good digestion and a bidet for your bottom. For all that, your heart was unsold. You smiled at the signposts of anguish as you passed through passion, into life. Where did you find guilt in this blameless adventure? And where did I find these whalebone words with which to light the censer?

Loss . . . they say the sense of loss is worst of all.

A stormtrooper (wounded) weeps in recognition of the yellow stain still visible in the snow, though frozen now. Memories blacken and erode further memories. There is no tragedy, only decay. ('But there can be no loss where there is no possession . . .'). A flower of sorts is dying while I hover, uncertain of whether to contemplate it or to pick it – and if I pick it, does it die any more on my account, does it seek an explanation?

Paris was a different matter. The evening was slovenly and hot, dripping around the raw thighs and inexpressible griefs of the day. It folded its wings and the real night gurgled from its beak. At the fountain in the square the débris and cocaine-memories of the afternoon littered the cobbles. The Hôtel Paradis. Upstairs in the collapsing light – amid the riots of a sodomised bed whose springs wailed with delight to hear his sobs; amid the hardening malevolence of spurted blood and sperm – a tendril of bruised love had crept away and crumbled in the ashtray. Sweat in my armpits; tears; shadows passing in the lost corridors of *demi-pension* . . . it could have happened fifty years ago. Some clichés never fade.

Once I travelled specially from London to Paris for alienated sex. A person called Denis, who had been in prison in Switzerland for paedophile atrocities, welcomed me to his dingy hotel room. I put my finger in his arse while trying to get his dick down my throat. 'It's dirty,' he said, wriggling further onto my finger. His crabs, which I imported to the UK, were dirtier.

I was never a drug-fiend's vice-zombie, just an ordinary boy up for adoption.

In the Bois de Boulogne a car stopped for me (who hitch-hikes at 3 a.m. in the Bois?). We did it against a tree. The other person was the type who moans in unspontaneous appreciation. He said, 'Tu baises bien.' It meant nothing to me.

Before they got wise to it, the fifth floor *Messieurs* in Printemps was a good place, much better than Harrods. A boy with a cockring and KY substitute (real KY, like real sex, is expensive in France) was compulsively surrendering himself to anyone who seemed to suggest (by what?) possession of a horsedick. He didn't want words or kisses. His arse was full of sperm, but he wanted more cock. MORE COCK!

A cheap hotel room in the rue d'Athènes with wallpaper on the doors and bathroom *en suite*, a thoughtful touch. A dark little boy on weekend furlough from his regiment fucked me very gently and with much tenderness. Perhaps these boys who fuck each other gently will inherit the earth. They – or their mothers and sisters who, by then, will be better equipped than us to deal with it.

The piss-house was in complete darkness; inside there was a row of silent men, a hint of furtive activity. There was one space, which I occupied. It wasn't so dark that the person standing next to me remained a total mystery. As my eyes adjusted, I could see that he was very young. His hand moved nervously towards my cock. I returned the compliment. Then I took his hand and squeezed it gently. I stroked his palm with my finger. It made me feel faint to be doing that there, where tenderness is forbidden. God knows what went through his mind. He took me to some flats nearby: graffiti, pissy smell, bits of rubbish, the usual; this isn't Harlem or Naples, it's London EC1 where the heroin is cheap, pure and plentiful and where even the softest lisp can sound barbaric.

We went to the top of the block, outside onto the roof. It was – a wonderful view . . . the smell of his smegma caught in my throat as he undid his pants. He drew me towards him, now visible as a dark Greek with Mediterranean eyes, and I got a whiff of his foetid breath just before the kiss. In disgust, I jerked off quickly, DIY. He looked disappointed, but did the same. Such a shame.

Perhaps such incidents would be less distressing if they happened on the quayside at Genoa or in a cardboard box in Trenchtown. Perhaps it would even seem romantic then, like Havana used to be . . . but what's really disturbing you is that almost all the possible world is either still unclaimed or already lost. Almost all you have left are my filthy memories – one interpretation of your exquisitely filthy dreams. Beneath the palm-tree of evening, in wicker chairs on some Malayan verandah, you propound riddles and smile, but not for long.

Part IV

Some pretty-boy from Brittany called Marc was a lover of mine in Paris. I remember him with a feeling of relief that it's over. I loathed the grunts and heavy exhalations, his clammy body arched in pre-orgasmic tension above me like a dog about to move its bowels. His ejaculations seemed to cause him pain. The spasms were always somehow strangled as they struggled through his muscles, as if he were trying to stop them from happening. He had spent seven years of his medical training in total abstinence, never once even jerking off. This, he said, had given him the energy to study. Any excuse, I thought.

He always had to be the big boy, the fucker. He had to be, so that he could be certain of having acted out the cliché of abusing me properly. He hated his sexual body and his homosexual desires so much that he couldn't even take it out on them directly. He couldn't acknowledge them except through me and all the others whom he was compelled to fuck while I knew him. He was the type who washes his dick the instant he's come. He prescribed drugs for himself to obscure his perpetual discomfort and gave drugs to me to justify his own addiction and to emphasise his power.

I eased myself away from him so delicately and considerately that he didn't even feel rejected. It was in the cafe at the Beaubourg. The worst thing was that I'd actually tried to love him.

The problems of the middle class are manifested in such an indirect way; it's part of their education. Having adopted for myself a déclassé approach, on the surface at least, I've learned to treat the bourgeoisie with the care they expect. It's more than they deserve, but it would be pointless to outrage them – just another move in the game which they always win (because the rules are theirs, and they change them according to their needs. Look at any post-revolutionary élite). I felt bad on my own account about showing this Marc creature so much consideration but even if I hadn't, the most that would have happened would have been some self-indulgent little middle-class guilt crisis on his part. Who needs their guilt? I operate somewhere outside their morality, but their almost effortless confidence and their unquestioning expectations make me hate them. The ones whose confidence is in crisis and whose expectations are tempered by some awareness of the nerve of it all are somehow even worse: social workers waiting for that delicious, expiating kick in the teeth. I'm too civilised for such small-scale violence and too aware of its other meanings; I'm not willing to show them my desperation. But as I drink their vulgar champagne and smile politely at their assumptions of moral certainty, a vestige of proletarian resentment churns my stomach. Do you know which knife to use for the pâté de foie? I know which knife to use. Isn't it outrageous to be eating pâté de foie in a squat? Yes, it is.

Another Marc was my lover once. He was a Jewish skinhead, a dope-fiend bike-boy who lived in a squat in Islington. I couldn't help noticing the catshit on the basement stairs, though I realised that, for him, its presence was irrelevant. Moreover, he was into *est* in a big way. He used to call Siegfried the 'schoolteacher', but he never met Janet – at least, not until the very last night of the affair. We fucked the daylights out of each other for a few weeks, but I began to find the drugs and the *est* a bit limiting. I told him over the phone that I'd had enough.

I should have remembered that phones are too impersonal. Two hours later, in the middle of the night, his flatmate phoned me to say that Marc was having a bad acid-trip. Janet and I went directly over, by taxi, to hold his hand through the night. Neither of us, I might add, have ever had any time for *est*.

Alex met Vincent in a bush at the Trocadéro. For weeks he fooled himself that this wasn't so significant – you have to meet Mr Right somewhere, so what's wrong with a bush?

I mistook Vincent for somebody else. Mr Right had actually just left and was on his way home on the Métro. But Vincent was so gorgeous that anybody would have made that mistake.

He had the right voice, the right muscles, the right dick, the right eyes. It was just his mind that wasn't right.

I don't think he wanted consciously to humiliate me. I didn't seek humiliation from him in any of the obvious ways. But if in some relationships the power seems to oscillate between each person to give some illusion of equality, with Vincent and me it was clear who was supposed to be the boss. Even though I intrigued him, it wasn't enough to shake his authority. He was the first person who ever tried to fistfuck me. I think the concept had just begun to be in vogue in Paris at the time. My feelings of vulnerability were allayed by his sweetness – his eyes were as soft as his tongue – despite his unequivocally brutal approach to my body. His physical brutality found its most extreme form in his jerk-off orgasm, leaving me to observe as he withdrew into himself to achieve an intimacy and an intensity which I could participate in only casually.

But it is with people like Vincent, whether I am infatuated with them or just willing to let them make decisions about my body, that I am able to forget Uncle Siegfried and Auntie Janet. If I didn't make time for that forgetting I would hardly exist. I create new memories to dislodge the old realities for a while; I manage the odd giggle beyond Siegfried's ironies and Janet's quiet smile.

I know it's not really very refined to have some huge dick jammed up your arse, but so what? At least it's a physical, knowable thing, not just a word. And at least, when the other person uses words such as 'I'm coming!', you know what they're talking about; when it's the other way round and you're plugged into someone else and they murmur 'Harder!', you know what they mean.

Who knows what anybody really means in other situations, where even words such as incest have lost a lot of their crisp, original clarity? These words are now just delicious, just little signs of weakness. But I never admitted that (unlike Andy, I had a reputation to think of) – I was always just escaping into Vincent's strong arms.

Vincent's arms could never embrace my Auntie Janet, which is why they were always so appealing, at least for as long as I could avoid thinking about why Auntie Janet would have made him so nervous. I could usually avoid it until he began to talk, in fact until he stopped behaving like an animal. His words betrayed a fear which was never expressed openly by his body (it was there, of course, but who thinks of such things in the middle of high sex?). His fears were personified in women and compounded by his confusion of his own lack of sexual desire for women with a general distaste for their company. Their presence in life threatened his tenuous grip on power; their frivolity shocked him; their strength and resilience made his muscles feel slack; he resented what he took to be their ability to transcend conflict. He was much happier when he was trying to fistfuck somebody like me and then pretending to achieve sexual and emotional autarky with the jerk of his manly wrist.

With Vincent I felt a certain relief to be away from Siegfried. It permitted me to be a little boy playing with a man's big hairy dick. And I felt a rather guilty pleasure in leaving Janet at home with the dishes. I was very much a *boy* for him – I had to be. He wouldn't have had anything to do with me if I'd had even the merest trace of hair on my chest; but conversely, if he'd caught me wearing mascara, he wouldn't have been too pleased either. It was OK for me to be the one who got up first and fetched the croissants, but it had to be his decision; and probably his money.

I can forget Siegfried and Janet sometimes, but it's so hard to forget power. Even Andy wouldn't let me do that very often. But I don't think I ever wanted Vincent to be powerful. In fact, I really didn't want that at all. It's just that it was either that or nothing, and at that time, anything was better than having to go home. He stopped seeing me when he realised I was shaving my chest.

It doesn't matter how sweet butch men can be, they're all fools.

Fear and power spiral around each other in unacknowledged intimacy, disguising our weaknesses as hate. You and I would both claim that there's no alternative, even though as children we knew differently, at least on some occasions. Lovers are so far from one's dreams that harshness grows like a man's beard or a hardening cock and smiles coldly at our terrors. But when you found me in tears and still chose to kiss me, the wicked little fingers of dream became for a moment sexless breaths passing wordlessly between us. There was no more need for jokes and fury.

Even if only for a moment, we knew then the difference between ourselves and these dreams of god which drag us apart.

It was a classic spring day on the boulevard St Germain; everybody was on the terraces, eyeing up everybody else. A wildly beautiful boy was drinking coffee as I walked past. I was quite hunky myself that day, the way people can be when they know they're in Paris with nothing to lose. The boy was dressed completely in white, not surprisingly.

After a certain amount of feigned window-shopping in which we both had the time to establish that an encounter was about to occur, he began to walk off, looking over his shoulder to check that I would follow. Then he disappeared into one of the university buildings. I went after him down about three flights of stairs into a basement that was in utter darkness. He grabbed me passionately, kissing, rubbing, tearing at my jeans. His dick was warm and very hard; his arse, slightly sweaty, was like he'd just that minute been fucked. He wouldn't let me speak. Afterwards, out on the street again, he smiled gorgeously, but never said a word. I watched him walking off, up towards the Panthéon, where I suppose he had his spiritual home.

Berlin is a cheap send-up of its own past (how much worse

can taste get than to present a photographic 'tribute' to concentration-camp victims in a rebuilt Reichstag? A major German contribution to American culture, apart from nuclear technology, is the difficulty experienced by the Establishment of both countries in understanding irony and in grasping the principles of good taste). Paris on the other hand is an ironic pastiche of itself which only gets out of hand when those elements of society that are prone to chauvinism start taking it all seriously. But in Paris the snobbish racists who cruise in the Tuileries with their Afghan hounds and the fragrance decreed for that season are still ultimately just ridiculous. They don't give me that feeling of uneasiness which so quickly establishes itself if I ever make the mistake of going to one of the Trollettes' mass rallies in those seedy South London pubs. It's not that Paris is any less worrying than other cities. It seethes with just as much violence and meanness; its queens can be just as disappointingly unworthy of themselves as any others; and in some sense the stench of luxury on the rue St Honoré is even more foul than elsewhere in the world because those who create it are so self-assured. But at least these phenomena exist within a context which manages to hold on to a certain elegance and which can still, occasionally, produce a splendour uncontaminated by the vulgarity (or is it just the mediocrity?) of this new universe. (I'm thinking mainly of the eyes of certain young men – North Africans, French proletarians, immigrants from the Antilles – eyes which express, however faintly, a trace of dignity which the city has perhaps unintentionally permitted them to retain. Look hard for that glimmer of dignity in the Cellar Bar. And I'm thinking too of those women who began to sing the *Internationale*, spontaneously, as the striking steel-workers of Lorraine marched past them on their way to the Place de la Concorde, just prior to the tear-gas and baton charge. Perhaps the tune is heard more often in Rome, but there are still a few French people who remember the words.)

But who am I trying to kid with this sentiment? The railway lines at Bobigny lead straight to Auschwitz. The City of Light is full of shadows.

I'm most consistently free of Janet and Siegfried in the most alienated of my sexual experiences. Their presence at times such as these would not only be *de trop*, it would have quite a deleterious effect on the development of the experience. Casual sexual partners (to use the jargon of the clinic and the consulting room without, I hope, implying the disapproval which its use in that context signifies) have no need of my uncles and aunts, any more than I have of theirs. For the duration of the fuck, the conventions, laws, and blood relatives of Western society are temporarily abolished. That's not to claim that the protagonists enter some kind of pure state, or that they come closer then to essentials than they would otherwise. Essence, whatever it may be, is hardly the concern of desire, no more than purity is a possible domain for existence. But still, any escape from taboos (and it's only ever temporary: order and chaos need each other), in fact any escape from anything is always subversive. It threatens the symmetry of beauty, but makes it more breathtaking; it uses power without drifting mindlessly into oppressiveness; although it's on a small scale, it's the only scale for hope.

If I stopped in a clearing and there was a man who was heavily built, though still young, standing near some trees, and if he was wearing a T-shirt and fatigues with his hair in a regulation crop, I could pull him towards me rather violently and kiss him. I could be his sex, pressing and rubbing against the surface (would it wither – its very ripeness the cruel condition of imminent decay?). I could kiss and bite my own lips in his sex. I could be his mouth, gorging myself on those rotting fruits, disgorging my despair onto the barbed wire of his slackening skin. My body; his sex; desire. Inseparable and clogged up in time. The images would break into fragments, but who would care in that momentary freedom? There would be power to be fought for and taken or relinquished, but without motives, neither of us caring what would happen, no moral imperatives to guide our actions, no theories of strength or potency to be proved. No words; only the soft sounds of an almost unexpected orgasm would remind us of words. I could hold his butt against my stomach afterwards until we disengaged, adjusted our clothing and parted. We wouldn't be worrying about equality or inequality. We would leave each other unrobbed and, for a while, content to be alone.

This new diary, the one that's possibly the margin of a real journal, is getting a bit out of order. But is that the fault of the miserable fucker who keeps it? A girl once said to me: 'You've got more mouth on you than a cow's got fanny, but you say fuck all.' Maybe she was right. The last entry is marked 'depraved': what's that supposed to mean? Siegfried told me off about it.

'The content of life may appear to be the important element,' he said, 'while the style can be almost overlooked, or neglected, as though it were not itself the content described differently. Just put the stress on the last syllable of "content" and see what happens.'

Here we go, I thought.

'Conversely, the style may be experienced acutely, irradiated by an intensity of significance which is inaccessible in the content. Perhaps style should be understood as content, and perhaps you should decide whether ennui and the creative energy which distorts it into pleasure is a function of content or of lack of content.' He was looking at me with triumph creeping into his bloodshot eyes. 'Or is it an emptiness of form and the desire to find another style which, for a while, may affect perception of experience so radically that boredom is temporarily vanquished?' It was a mystery to me where he dragged it all up from, especially since he's always half-pissed. I was wondering what the girl would have said about Siegfried.

'So this diary,' he droned on, 'these memories and ponderings collected here – do they describe dramatic events in some personal history: insights and probings in a coherent mind? Or are they an exercise in aesthetics by which to recognise not a person but an attempt at survival?

'This mass of detail which is often so inadequate and in a way so arbitrary is almost as irrelevant to you as it is to me. Hundreds of people have similar memories and parallel agonies of despair. Who cares for these anecdotes and identity-cries? What's the point in your mentioning this dick, especially if you're not going to bother with that one? I think it's just that this is a nearly-new outfit which you're determined to wear at least once. But it's unclear whether the pleasure in wearing it is private or public – some transvestites stay at home, others go prancing round the streets, but with you, who knows? It's also unclear if it's the outfit that defines the wearer or if the wearer is simply modelling the outfit. This little ensemble is a surface between us – a barricade perhaps or a fly to be unbuttoned or an uncoordinated shambles of accessories which nobody else would be seen dead in.'

He paused briefly and then, with unconvincing nonchalance, he played his trump: 'I have no doubt that you'll alter it when the novelty has worn off.'

We have to try and respect our ancestors.

Part V

The narratives of desire have no beginning. There is only an endless past marked with memories of escape – or is it transformation? These memories are the moments of love. Between that non-beginning and the unimaginable ending are these moments of delicious loss. No mortal self or mortal other . . . but almost immediately it becomes some kind of agony.

The deathless moments are those when lives and images collude in an irrational present, a suspension of past and future beyond memory and understanding. Can you believe that this is the only respite? The rest is this interminable story, this dialogue with memory which can never be concluded.

You and I have struggled to create a series of images which can serve as a faith. The words we use may have their meanings and their absences of meaning, speaking tenderly to us, pleading for hope. But now - it's already reached this stage – these words of ours lie electrocuted beneath the wicker chairs. The air is growing cooler. We are in the *jardin d'hiver*, where the evening spreads like a velvet palm-tree. Our eloquence has already begun to slide into silence.

So delightful.

Christoff, a would-be aristocrat, used to wet me with his tongue before buggering me. That may have been the first time I felt someone's tongue between my legs, a first experience of that intimate sensation. It was long before the hepatitis scare – in a hunting lodge in Heidelberg, in fact. The violence of his cock-thrusts was all the more disorienting after those initial soft probings of his tongue and the slight roughness of his cheek against my skin.

I met Nino in Trafalgar Square. He was half-African, from the Canary Islands. I took him to see a subtitled version of *Satyricon* in Leicester Square. (He still hadn't fully come to terms with the implications of our meeting. I thought it might reassure him to see debauchery on the screen.) He came home with me and fucked me, but wasn't quite sure whether he should enjoy it. When I met him again, about a year later, he was loitering around the Boltons in tight jeans. He'd invested in a nancy haircut. He no longer talked in Spanish about his girlfriends. When we got home he undressed and immediately lay on the bed on his stomach. 'Fuck me,' he said in English, and relaxed into his favourite position.

'I don't know why you don't find yourself a nice young man and settle down,' said Auntie Janet, as she poured Alex his coffee. (She knew, even if he didn't, that there was a hint of irony in her words.) Alex had been complaining to her about his life in London, slagging off the clubs and the people who haunted them. Janet's perspective on clubs was slightly different. Her only contact with nightlife these days was through her friend Gertie who had worked for a while as a cleaner in a pub-disco in Islington. She knew, thanks to Gertie, what went on in such places; she even knew that the boys had drug-crazed sex together in the toilets (leaving the mess for somebody else to clean up); and it seemed to her that if you participated in such experiences you would eventually become distressed by them, which was why she sometimes worried about Alex. But equally, she understood that if you didn't participate, whether involuntarily or by choice, then the risk to your state of mind was ultimately no less alarming. For Janet, it wasn't enough to complain about these places; it was more a question of removing the need to frequent them. And obviously by far the best method of achieving this was to find a steady, loyal date who liked giving dinner-parties or going to the cinema.

Alex found his aunt's magical solutions to ennui a little wearing.

'Do you actually believe that I'm going to find Mr Right?' he asked. 'And in any case, if he existed, where else would I find him but in a nightclub?'

Janet took off her pinnie, the one a friend had made her for Christmas with 'Macho Man' sewn in black sequins on the front (although she quite liked this garment, she wasn't sure of its significance). She sat down for the first time that day, taking the weight off her feet.

'I'm not suggesting that you go to a nightclub to look for a boyfriend, and I'm certainly not talking about Mr Right. I'm talking about settling down. You do that by compromising a little bit. It's the only way.'

What Janet didn't understand was that boyfriends, unfortunately, are not girlfriends with dicks. Alex was exasperated. Out of spite, he went and got a number one crop down at the barber's, hunted out his oldest, tightest denims and some braces, and polished his DM's. (It was still possible in those days for Alex to adopt the style of a skinhead without feeling utterly uncomfortable.)

However, later that night at the pub he lost all this carefully-applied poise within seconds when a young man – Andy – smiled at him as they waited their turn at the bar.

'Can you offer me a place in your life, or only in your memory?'

After some time, about a year, Andy decided that he wanted to do something about himself, but he felt he'd never be able to do it while he was with Alex. It's unfortunate that one of the aspects of exploring one's own needs is the realisation that one is seldom appropriately placed for their fulfillment.

Alex was afraid of admitting openly that his life hadn't been very fulfilled, and he kept it to himself until almost the very day that Andy left. But on that day he fulfilled at least his need to shed tears.

He was also afraid of loving and respecting Andy, but to his credit, he never said anything like 'I didn't realise until it was too late', partly because he suspected that he would never have allowed himself to 'realise' anything very much precisely until it was 'too late', and partly because, in secret, he loved and respected him without qualification.

When Andy made this move, I was hoping that he wouldn't abandon that original faith in his own and other people's feelings which he'd had when we first met, and which, even though I knew it made him suffer, had astonished and humbled me. This faith was an almost incoherent awareness that he had, not something that can be expressed in formulae or that can be found in books or experiences by those who don't have it. I was scared, I suppose, that in doing something about himself, he would lose that innocence and suffer even more. Sadly, I knew how fragile it was.

'Only in my memory . . .'

Change, development and disappearance remind you that eternity doesn't exist, that your beliefs and feelings are unstable. Perhaps only those who can no longer face growth and who have chosen to wait for death can pretend that they have escaped time – until death itself calls the bluff. But it's in the passing of time and situations that pain and grief emerge. With each development and disappearance – each growth – the yearning for eternity in life becomes more painful. The pain changes, too, and diminishes. The only thing you can count on is that it will never disappear for good. Andy never hurt me; I did the damage myself, with memories.

One night a notorious personage took me home to get fucked. It was the night of the legendary Gay Pride débâcle when Myra Mugshot had been arrested, among others, for wearing a meat-cleaver in her hat. Many years before, the personage had pressed himself against me in the Coleherne (I was still just a chicken) and later, round the corner at the Catacombs, he'd cruised me the way people used to in those days (now they just grab your dick when you're having a piss at Heaven). I hadn't known him then and for some reason I hadn't gone home with him, even though he was no dog. Then, some time later while I was working as a theatre telephonist on an old doll's-eye board, I'd observed him daily when he came in to use the pay-phone near my desk. He was going through a nancier phase by then, like most of us do. The reason he was using the phone was because he was setting up the deal that was going to make him notorious. One time, not recognising me from the Catacombs, he slipped me a piece of paper with his address on it and invited me to a party there. I didn't go.

Anyway, that night, everyone was at the university, getting drunk and dancing and feeling pleased with themselves for having kneed a few coppers in the balls. (The British police force is actually the worst in the world, not for its violence, which is probably not as extensive as that of some others, but for its grotesque hypocrisy. We loved the unhypocritical feeling of our kneebones grinding into their flesh, even if we were just a bunch of privileged radicals.) The personage offered me a spliff, needless to say without the faintest glimmer of recognition in his eyes. Soon we were back at his flat; a new manuscript was tossed carelessly on the table, the bed, still unmade, smelt of an even more notorious personage than him. He had dispensed with the nanciness by this time; he was a hundred percent art-clone by now. He fucked me rigid and mercilessly, pushing my face into the pillow when not jerking it back and stuffing poppers up my nose. I gasped appropriately. Sometimes when I've seen him around he still tries to cruise me, utterly and almost pathetically unaware that he's already had it up me. But despite this I respect him. He may be cynical of the subculture, but somewhere he still has some faith, not just in himself.

Ralph was a physical scandal: a young Anglo-Caribbean with massive eyes, little white teeth, a downy moustache and an extremely cute rear-end. Two spliffs and a couple of hits of amyl helped us to melt together for an hour or so. It was a face-to-face fuck with a continuous kiss. Later we jerked off together, lapping up each other's spurts to show we weren't being selfish, each snuggling afterwards into the other's dampness; we held each other gently, but our muscles were firm enough to remind us that we were both still young.

I don't think I'll ever be the type to stuff hamsters up my arse (or anyone else's); there's a certain eclecticism about my own extravagances. Food, livestock, and the more sophisticated sort of appliance would generally find no place in my activities. Is it a failure of the imagination or just a function of my honeysuckle childhood?

A full-moon entry in the new diary remarks: 'Call *that* sex? Fags, Alcohol, Sex, Drugs, Sex.' Well, yes I would call *that* sex, even though the entire operation was performed with a lavatory wall between me and my partner. He was tall, dark and extremely handsome. His moustache made him look about thirty-five. He was kneeling on the floor in the next cubicle. I could just see enough to know that he had a whopper. His legs were very hairy and still tanned even though it was winter. He wanted me to push my finger up his arse while he jerked himself off. I obliged and his sperm landed on my arm, soaking into the tattered leather sleeve. Because he looked so respectable and so classically masculine, I felt a *frisson*, a sense of mischievous transgression, at what I was doing. I had to go home and jerk off immediately so that I didn't lose any details. The jerk-off memories make incidents into small crystals of experience before they dissolve into the anti-matter of everyday reality. Even the most tenuous incidents like this one can become essential to the construction of those principles on which the rest of one's life is founded.

Later that day I had two further, apparently more substantial though infinitely less noteworthy sexual encounters; one was with some Norwegian clone, the other with a nancy-boy. They both fucked me. It was on that evening too that the notorious personage bought me a drink. Naturally, he didn't have a clue who I was. In the course of conversation he suggested that we become friends (maybe I was getting too old to be fuckable). I accepted – but if we do, shall I ever tell him who he is?

'It's all very well for us,' said Uncle Siegfried. They were in some straight pub somewhere, by far the best place for a drink and a chat, since the number of distractions was minimal (who wants to fuck even the most fabulous straight man?). 'It's all very well being bohemian – radical – intellectual – artistic – however you want to put it; we can get away with that because we know we're marginalised and we even enjoy that knowledge to some extent. You've only got to look at yourself.' It was he in fact who was looking at Alex. 'There you are with your *outré* hairstyle, your sex-clothes, your earrings, your occasional bits of make-up, enjoying the risk of distinguishing yourself from others.'

'But I don't enjoy being intimidated on the street because of how I choose to look,' said Alex.

'Nobody is secure on the street, though perhaps some are even less secure than others. But that's not quite my point. What I'm saying is that the celebration of diversity is a kind of perverse, apocalyptic luxury. It's something which most other people can't permit themselves – or only very slightly. And that's not just because they're afraid of being attacked like budgerigars among a flock of gabble-ratchers, it's because they believe that they've still got more to lose than us . . . It's like being "apolitical" or philistine: those attitudes are inevitably reactionary, but the fear that encourages them is well-grounded. We may fear the physical violence of mentally retarded skinheads . . .' he paused momentarily for Alex to savour this phrase, 'but when the Italians stared at our bleach-jobs, we actually found it quite delectable. We bleached our hair to fuck *on purpose*. Doesn't that strike you as rather sick?'

I knew what he meant, but I wasn't sure that it actually applied well to the facts. I'm no alternative Miss World. When I went to have a piss, I looked at myself in the mirror. Vestiges of bleached hair gelled into a curl at the front of my otherwise near-shaved head; a couple of quite discreet and unostentatious earrings; a black outfit, slightly militarist, held together by studded belt, chain, wristband, braces; scuffed and well-worn work-boots – in other words, little different from hundreds of others that year (it may have been 1982), leatherised, chained, hinting at an army-surplus never-tomaterialise S&M. Wasn't I just a failed clone, one cast of a rather limited edition that's been made available to collectors of camp-trash ephemera? Siegfried secretly wanted me to be a one-off – if nothing else, he still had faith in originality, even if it was a desperate, self-conscious faith – but I was too absorbed in the ceremonies of self-objectification: I was far too bothered about love and sex to be really devoted to art. In every mirror I wanted to see the image of a man, but usually I only ever found evidence of my own failure to effect the magical transformation. Just because of who I was and where I was, I was participating in this ridiculous post-Romantic aesthetics of identity, but it was actually no more for me than a discourse with my own desires.

Later that night we went to the Palace to be seen. We also saw: the usual few 'stars', the couple of hundred over-familiar habitués, the rare new face. Siegfried spent most of the night making polite, amusing conversation with people to whom it was necessary to talk. He, the notorious marginal, is nevertheless quite an old-style opportunist when it comes to exploring the possibilities of alternatives to an *obscure* marginalisation. He'd rather be respected than loved, I think.

I was with him most of the time. Occasionally, I'd slink off into the shadows, or sometimes dance. I met someone who once gave me a very boring fuck, a German boy with an unremarkable interest in S&M. I watched a couple of fantasies for a while, one quasi-straight and famous, the other a queer nobody, but both of them were busily wasting their time on other people. I realised, as I invariably do at about one-thirty in fashion-clubs, that I should have been on the Heath instead. It's at about that time that I begin to feel like an adolescent with an inexplicably and permanently stiff dick, despite actually looking more like a tired gatecrasher who's a bit the worse for wear with drink.

Clemens and I hardly ever spent much time in clubs, though I think we both had the impression that we did. Most weekends I went to the half-way house for schizophrenics in the country which was where he worked. Our nights were always threatened with the possibility of disruption – someone jumping out of the window or slashing what was left of their wrists in the bathroom. The residents always chose the least convenient moments to stage their dramas. It reassured them, I suppose, that they were always more of an attraction for the workers than boyfriends could ever be.

Clemens would have liked to fall in love with me, but I wouldn't let him. We went to Venice for the weekend and there, by a canal at about two in the morning, I told him we'd better not have sex anymore. We did, but only once, and that was over a year later. It was the best sex we ever had.

There was a tough-looking man wearing a green cover-all over his sweaty T-shirt. I put my hand inside and touched his arse. He pulled away at first, but then relented and let me go ahead. We went back to my place.

He told me he'd never let anyone touch him there before and he wasn't sure why he'd permitted it now (who cares whether it was the truth; images exist, that's enough). He wanted rough sex, naturally. He couldn't handle tenderness in case it made him feel unmanly (you can even let a boy poke your arsehole, but you must never kiss him). I watched him jerk himself off, lying on the floor, still wearing his boring DMs. He was dirty-talking, unable to choose between admiring his own dick and looking at me as I 'caught' him being naughty. I had the faint suspicion that he was a copper, but I didn't ask. In any case, it was the concretisation of a junior jerk-off fantasy I'd had when I was about eleven, before I'd graduated into 'real' experience. That's what makes it important. I'd imagined opening the door of a lock-up cubicle in some provincial Gents and finding a man – this man – jerking off. He had to be over thirty with dark hair and a moustache and a mean sort of face, and he had to be jerking *himself* off: that was the central point. I suppose I felt that real grown-up men wouldn't do that type of thing.

So I watched this man with delight, but I couldn't help feeling some contempt for him. He was only there, permitting me this honour, because he'd decided that he had some respect for me, enought to let me touch his arse. In other words, he didn't perceive me as a queen; he could allow himself to imagine that he was at the army base or in the locker room experiencing a wholesome masculine jerk-off with a straight buddy. The buddy was butch enough not to give him by implication any disquieting thoughts about that terrifying queen who may be lurking within. I didn't tell him, of course, but I knew that she *was* lurking within. It's pathetic.

I think that's what's so attractive about the idea of fucking butch men. There's an obverse attraction about getting fucked by boys.

My first glimpse of Albert was a rear-view. He was pissing into some bushes, dressed in white. His cock was just right. We fucked each other each time we happened to meet. The details are so insubstantial, really so straightforward, but he's a favourite memory: boy-sex without butch and bitch or, seen from another perspective, with a bit of both . . .

Part VI

Was that I in a leather-bar in Montmartre ? Upstairs in the fuck-room I couldn't fail to notice an Arab being eaten by a young French leather-boy. When the latter had had enough, the Arab was left standing there, apparently unsure of what to do next with his glistening cock. I went over and made some suggestions. Then we went home for total sex. As he pushed his dick in (I made no protestations, submitting myself to the dictates of his culture as though the lessons I had learnt from my own were now somehow invalid), he whispered gently in my ear: 'I hope it's not too big for you.' Even the gentlest dirty talk is sometimes addressed primarily to oneself.

Was that I one night in Tufnell Park, hitching a ride even though I only lived in Highgate? An Indian stopped, and I got in. He didn't bother to ask me where I was going; he just inquired: 'Are you into kinky sex?' 'Yes,' I said, with remarkable presence of mind. He drove me back to his flat, the walls of which were attractively decorated with tasteful prints and various instruments of torture. I felt apprehensive, not yet having managed to work out who was to take which role. I hoped for once that we weren't going to have any silly nonsense about power-sharing. Instinct told me that if I simply assumed a role as though it were the sort of thing I always did then everything would follow in that direction. Fortunately this turned out to be the case. Having opted to be the master, I informed my slave that we wouldn't be using any of the 'gear' and told him to get undressed and lie on his stomach. While I was fucking him, I got hold of his fringe and banged his head against the wall. It made me feel sick – I was in danger of losing my hard-on. He moaned, ambiguously. 'Did you enjoy that? Tell me you enjoyed that!' I commanded him, amazed at myself. He didn't answer so I did it again. 'Tell me you enjoyed that, bitch!' 'No,' he groaned, 'please don't.' He was pushing up against me so hard that I thought my dick was going to damage him. I carried on servicing him in the detached passionless way of the true non-sadist. Eventually, after what seemed like ages, each thud becoming more mechanical, I felt his butt squirming in orgasm beneath me. I didn't come. So why do I bother to remember it?

Yes, it was I, but I was pretty bored by it. Of course, it was before the new wave of S&M, it was even before Guilt, so I didn't worry too much. I had no analyses with which to just about anchor me to my body. The church, the class struggle, theatre, the politics of trust – none of these came into it in those days, though perhaps some people even then, even as flesh slapped flesh, were under threat of being dragged off into dreamland by the idea of it all.

But boredom shouldn't be confused with 'boredom', which is the word used by urbane moralists when they justify their condemnation of the pornographic and the perverse in that sneaky-sophisticated way of theirs. No, it's just the boredom of a poor boy in a swanky hotel, an ennui which is easily mistaken, even by the one who feels it, for awe: it's hard to identify the truth of the feeling because one's poor-boy values are rarely acknowledged enough by others or by oneself to be able to recognise their real class. The poor would have good taste if it weren't for the subversions of the middle class. Who would think of buying fish-fingers if they weren't practically forced into it by the people who want to make a fortune out of selling processed cod? Who would aspire to drinking cocktails at the Algonquin with some of the most grotesque dogs on earth if they really thought lucidly about it? Whose mind would it cross to truss up one's sex-partner like a chicken and whip the shit out of them for fun if middle-class men hadn't infected the whole world with their views, which reduce everything to questions of power? The only way there'll ever be a radical change in the world will be when people start refusing to interpret their whole life in terms of power over others or of others' power over them. In the meantime, let them rationalise fist-fucking as an exercise in trust; it's no worse than all the rest.

And the people who *want* to be ass-whipped by the Ku-Klux-Klan? Before I can think of an answer to that, my safeword tenderly escorts me into a different frame of mind.

Unfortunately, Uncle Siegfried wouldn't let me escape that easily. 'Faggots are involuntary rebels,' he said, as soon as I let him catch me off-guard. His expression was as if he'd just said something scandalously original. I fixed his drink and waited for the inevitable thesis. He began by changing the subject. He does it on purpose.

'The structure of society demands that communication be substituted by a discourse between authority and submission or rebellion. This is the actual dialogue which occurs in sex. In a way, S&M queens participate as radicals in that dialogue, both among themselves and with others. Their rites are confrontations with power. They play with images of power quite openly.'

'You once said you thought S&M was about religious guilt and love-*transferts* in the bourgeois context!' I remarked with a hint of triumph.

'That doesn't mean,' snapped Siegfried, looking mysterious, 'that I don't have other thoughts on the subject. When I was talking about guilt, I was looking at it from another perspective.' He was on spirits that evening. I watched him inhale the Delphic vapours.

'Unlike cultural minorities whose relationship with authority, whether internal or external, is at least perceptible,' he went on, 'faggots grow up with no reference points which are particular to themselves. For most of our early lives, we either don't know we're lepers or if we do, we don't know *why*.' I noticed that he'd started saying 'faggot'. I suppose it sounds better than some of those more political words. 'Which is why I think ritual streetsex becomes so central to the experience of a lot of faggots. Rites establish where you stand and by implication who you are. The reduction of identity to social position – to power-relations – is almost inevitable in this culture.

'Although all faggots are rebellious in the sense that the forms of expressing their desire are consciously unorthodox, within their relationships the old hierarchies are reconstituted: the butch-bitch syndrome. This avoids total anarchy in faggot-sex much as anarchy is avoided generally. I don't know what this says about mass-psychology. It may be a question of confidence or of responding to a system which survives on a myth of Order . . . looking at it pessimistically, which I sometimes do, you could say that there will always be powerful people and submissive people with a few rebels thrown in for excitement. Or you could see it more optimistically and hope that at some stage somebody will begin to operate outside of that system and that their ideas will catch on – everyone in control of themselves but no-one in control of anyone else. . . .'

I felt he was running out of steam. 'What about the people whose roles aren't stabilised?' I asked politely.

'In every sexual act, the roles are there, even if the participants alternate between them. But in my experience, it's quite unusual to find a partner who can deal with that ambiguity. That's why I mentioned S&M.' He paused again as though unsure of what should come next. Then, suddenly, Pythia was back on her tripod. 'Of course some people have argued that to see sex in terms of butch and bitch is necessarily reactionary and somehow irrelevant. As though the *kernel* of Western sexual experience could possibly be irrelevant . . . there was all that early-Seventies nonsense where people actually avoided anal sex. They must have thought that by pretending not to have roles they'd magically transcend the whole problem. They behaved as though a social and economic revolution had already happened . . . but S&M queens are pushing the roles to an extreme; and the fact that's it's often in S&M that the roles are most clearly swapped is extremely interesting.

'If you fuck butch men to challenge their authority, even if you also want them to fuck you, it's only subversive within its own logic: it doesn't go beyond rebellion. In some ways it just confirms the concept of hierarchy. It's the same if you encourage boys to fuck you, even if you also want to fuck them (and let's face it, who doesn't?) But in S&M the game can be played at a much less obscure level where it's possible to be the boss, the rebel and the submissive queen virtually simultaneously. The whole business of the desire for power and the desire to submit to it or to challenge it are thrown into question, which may not be much but it's something. The drawback, I find, is that tenderness and compassion can easily be lost in the violence of those questions. That unsettles me. But perhaps in a culture where order and authority are so fundamental, it's ultimately quite logical that tenderness should lose out. After all, tenderness is a kind of mutal yielding which is quite out of keeping with the forms of most non-sexual relations. It's extraordinary, I think (and perhaps it should encourage us), that people still manage to fall in love.'

'Isn't what you're saying a little bit phallocentric?' I remarked. He looked at me balefully. I realised that the conversation had come to an end.

Michael tore the integument of his uncut dick while he was fucking me. There was blood everywhere. It was sticky between my legs. At first we thought he'd lacerated me internally. Then he smiled his exquisite Franco-Indian smile and began to dab himself with Kleenex. The queen on night duty in the casualty department tidied him up and told him not to be so rough in future, her imagination running riot.

The next time we met he was behaving like Brer Rabbit. Ostensibly he still wanted to fuck me, but I knew he was really waiting for me to insist on doing it the other way round (that way – not his suggestion – it wouldn't look so bad). He was no virgin. He pushed back against me firmly and I could feel the smoothness of our whole bodies pressed together. The nerve-endings seemed more than usually sensitive. I had that secure feeling that we fitted together perfectly.

Later he joined the army. When he came home on leave, he was full of forces nonsense and fake camaraderie. He still wanted my cock, but it wasn't quite the same kick for me. Even though I knew he'd been corrupted, I couldn't quite forgive him for having allowed it to happen.

Since then I've only seen him once, haunting a bar, looking older and rather jaded, searching for a really *big* one. I remember him, but only just.

Auntie Janet's memories are not the same as mine, though perhaps they have a similar function. In some ways, she's always been old, and her memories of youth are really not so much based on experience as on a kind of elaborated transmutation of the past. Maybe that's why she always refers to herself and her friends as 'girls'. She knows how much certain feminists would take exception to this so she's rather circumspect in her use of it, but in her mind she *is* a girl – a rather unfortunate girl, yes, but one who is nevertheless unwilling to accept that her present circumstances must necessarily define what she calls her soul. Circumstances took most of Africa from the slaves, but not quite all of it. If she were a New Yorker instead of a Londoner, she would use 'girls' as a vocative in the same way that Claudette Colbert probably did in one of her less remarkable films. It's much nearer to respectable East End than to Angela Brazil; but more important than that, it's an expression of Janet's ironic faith in the power of the word – a faith (or a sense of irony) which has nothing in common with the fundamentalist politics of modern times. In a way she admires the certainty of those who have thrown away their heels and lipsticks and taken to wearing dungarees, riding a bicycle, soaking beans and having as little as possible to do with men, but she knows she'd never feel comfortable in that world. It's a world which secretly appals her, not for its dreams but for its insensitivity, especially its poor choice of words. When they speak of celibacy and political lesbianism, don't they realise that she, Janet, has never had sex with men – with anyone – anyway? Don't they realise that her life is a triumph – well, a Pyrrhic victory – over sex? Don't they understand that she, a deferential working-class woman at heart, suffers almost as much from that sort of language as from her actual position in the world? But deference brings resignation, and besides being resigned to her place at the sink (where she's been dreaming of glamour ever since Harold Wilson was elected), she's also resigned to being inadvertently betrayed by her would-be sisters, the ones who had the time, the money and the opportunity to stop dreaming and to start burning their bras or to shoot Andy Warhol. Suffering and dreaming are so wonderfully non-analytical, like the way that crow's feet show up in neon light no matter what you've slapped on your face. Analysis, like collagen-implants, is another world.

Sometimes, when Siegfried has gone on a binge and we're alone, she'll talk to me of her memories, hesitantly, always afraid of not saying quite what I want to hear. Listening to them, I feel slightly uncomfortable, partly because there's something rather tragic in the way she recalls even the most hilarious incidents and partly, too, because I sense in these accounts a naiveté which is oddly familiar to me despite my streetwise life. What's most endearing about Janet is that she doesn't even try to make out that these past events form a coherent story. They are retold as a series of rather bewildering non-sequiturs, adventures which are still a bit of a mystery, even to her. Life for Auntie Janet has no particular etiology, and her current identity, though perceived clearly by those who know her, makes no claims at self-definition. She's too grown-up to need to make sense of herself.

Like some tragedy-queen she enjoys thinking of what she might have been, but the difference is that she doesn't really resent being who she is now. She has faith, or as some would put it: class, style, integrity . . .

Andy's collection of self-portraits is similar to my old go-down of memories. He photographs himself endlessly in any number of poses, hair-cuts, make-up jobs and outfits (the attire, however informal, is usually correct). The camera desires him without requiring reciprocal arrangements. It provides him with those terms of his image from which definitions can be constructed, even if only to be thrown away immediately. His vulnerable side is always there, asking for kisses. Some people call it paranoia – as though their own identities were stabilised and fixed without the intervention of a lens; as though their identities were never undermined by the power of other people to see what they want; as though they never mistook desiring eyes for those of the persecutor.

He keeps the pictures in a washbag; they travel with him like documentary evidence to prove that he belongs to the world. It's more than an identity card, but I think he knows that it's insubstantial evidence. They are really images of his absence from the world, icons of a faith he's not sure he'll ever believe in.

Sex-memories are equally open to doubt. But aren't they more than jerk-off numbers? Or rather, isn't jerking off more than just a way of evacuating the heart? The camera momentarily permits Andy to exist ideally. Jerking off allows Alex his moment of ideal vulnerability. If it were possible, that's one of the ways he'd like to exist.

Memory is the power to control the past. In memory a young boy allows me to stop being reliable, and yet he feels no contempt; he becomes strong for me and for himself, in control of his desire. I know it's unlikely. In memory an older man allows me to stop rebelling, but he doesn't carve another notch on his belt; he becomes vulnerable for us both, but not pathetic. Maybe that's less unlikely. These sex-memories select moments of freedom from the story of a desperate attempt at mere survival.

The act of taking pictures is as ritualistic as sex. The act of looking at them is as perverse and comforting as sex-remembrance: as though at those times it were possible to control more than the past. Andy listened to my memories and was scared. I remained with a few photographs of him and other strangers.

A provincial encounter: a very handsome young man took me behind some ever-convenient bushes and asked me what my preference was. I panicked at the thought of giving an answer which might put him off (it was relative, not absolute desperation: I wanted *him*, even though I knew there were others who were willing to have me regardless of my tastes).

I made a snap decision and said that I liked being fucked. 'Good,' he said enthusiastically, 'I like fucking.' Know your place, it's so much simpler.

His looks and the warmth of his body seemed incongruous in some bit of urban scrubland, but he fucked me silly anyway. He was in such good shape that it made me feel like a mess.

Ron was a real mess. A cynical, failed impresario. He pushed his oversized bulge against me as he squeezed past to go for a piss. I loathed him. We were in the Black Cap at the time when it was still a flesh-pot. I fell for Tom immediately, and somehow I managed to get him home with me without Ron. They were both drunk enough not to care. Tom was my first bleach-queen. His hair was like fibreglass but I sensed that it was just a superficial problem. He wrapped his legs around me and pulled me so close into him that my cock really was banged right up his arse to the balls. He still wanted more and he wanted it more brutal.

I courted him for weeks afterwards, but we never fucked again. I didn't realise at the time that he just wasn't interested in my vanilla approach. I didn't understand that that was why he found the little creep with the big dick so irresistible, but only wanted to discuss shampoos for damaged hair with me. Even so, I still have copies of his poems.

Nostalgia for lovers and the frantic rummaging through these piles of old sex-memories: both are so detached, but so much a part of this culture of acquisition and possession. Lovers tell you a hundred times of their love but it isn't enough, especially when it's over. Hundreds of people gobble your cock, but that's never enough either. Which mouth do you trust the most – the one with words and kisses or the one that's mute and full of your sperm? Both will forsake you . . . won't they?

Loss dribbles between us like sleep and neither of us can know whose is the greater loss. I stand at the bar with Andy and Claire, a year to the day after I broke my watch, losing my sense of time. The place was a thousand miles away, in

Rome, an hour ahead of Greenwich. My watch stopped then, this day a year ago, and when I came home, feeling at last that it was time to love him, he was gone. Now he's here with me and Claire, and it's time for me to leave. There's another person here too who once filled his mouth with my memory. It's time for me to leave. Each of them is lost in fragments of thought. They are waiting – still – to be found . . . but not in my memory tonight.

Part VII

Amsterdam, Vienna, Berlin, Paris, Rome and all the other cities have passed like dreams. London, the home of Auntie Janet and the place in which Uncle Siegfried has settled for a marginalisation which sometimes verges on the cosy, is probably as good as anywhere for Alex these days; it's a combination of the familiar and the ever-foreign, only dreary for him when his fear makes him dream of paradise.

Auntie Janet lives on a pre-War council estate in South London, a rather delapidated slum. But she's tried to make it comfortable inside, at least. In her younger days she always lived in North London, but that was before certain key parts of it started to be overwhelmed by the presence of the street-cool bourgeoisie, the vulgarity of whose colonies has to be tolerated under the name of inner-urban regeneration but who, Janet feels, are best left to neighbour each other if possible. Siegfried was always in his element in the North London era, however naff the actual accommodation may have been. Alex liked it too: being able to walk on the Heath in the afternoon, chattering to Siegfried about meanings and meaninglessness, or in the evening, still on the Heath but alone, at the hour when philosophy becomes less urgent. It wasn't just the topography of North London that appealed; the atmosphere itself was as stimulating as England ever can be.

Not that any of them would ever have countenanced a life in Tottenham or Finchley or, Heaven forbid, Willesden. North London to them meant that arc of sub-metropolitan (and unfortunately eminently gentrifiable) land which stretches roughly from Chalk Farm to Stoke Newington. Anything north of Archway, anything verging on the

Crouch End or the Swiss Cottage was beyond the pale. However, their real horror was, and still is West London. Siegfried described it once as an 'arid suburb full of late-night grocer's shops and desperate bedsits'. There may be more to it than that, but none of them was interested. Alex loathed Holland Walk.

While living in North London (Alex and his uncle always stayed with Janet between adventures), they had a certain amount of interesting contact with the East End, but virtually none at all with the South. When the Shoreditch skins were singing 'South of the Border, down Bermondsey way', Alex had some appreciation of their feelings, even if he didn't share their territorial neuroses. The South seemed forbidding and mournful, somewhere drab to pass through on occasional trips to Brighton or on the way to Dover.

So it was something of a shock to the system when Uncle Siegfried and I returned from Rome and found ourselves not at home but in somebody else's ghetto, a place where the assertion of black manhood bristles uneasily among the squalid agonies of the white trash, a place where the church-hats of Jamaican mothers and the cadences of Walworth spivs are still only slightly criticised by the affluence of Clapham Common and Dulwich Village.

We both settled in quite quickly, each too familiar with foreign parts to be disoriented for long by the transthamesian wilderness. And perhaps Andy's arrival helped in that, although it also had its disadvantages. The flat became extremely overcrowded, jammed full of people and all their lost property. The situation wasn't helped by Siegfried's insistence on acquiring junk-furniture (his way of acknowledging that the end may be nigh) – Janet's few possessions weren't really adequate for the four of us; she'd managed before on the bits and pieces her mother had given her, and which with a knowing smile she called her 'trousseau', but even the best appointed bottom-drawer wouldn't have provided enough for us all. So we ended up living in a pile of rubbish which Janet and Andy somehow disguised as a home.

Now there are just the three of us again. In theory, anyway. The remnants of Andy's presence sometimes catch me off-guard: his book of medical terminology, abandoned and shoved under the bed; his skateboard behind the wardrobe; hair-dye stains down the side of the bath. I still sleep in my 'half' of the bed even when there's no-one else in it, but especially when there is. Janet doesn't do so much cooking and cleaning since he left. She says it doesn't seem worth it, as though Siegfried and I didn't count. But, oddly enough, it was Uncle Siegfried of the three of us who was hardest hit by Andy's flit.

My diary at the time of Siegfried's breakdown was neither from the People's Republic nor in the form of a public wall chart. It was a pocket-size desk diary of the type favoured by aspiring administrators. It's only quite recently that I've taken to using Janet's kitchen as a Wall of Democracy. The desk diary is mainly just a record of the dates of Auntie Janet's entertainments. Not long after we got back from Rome and up to the time when Andy left, she'd gone through a period of intensive catering. She called these evenings her 'at homes', remembering the traditions of provincial lady mayoresses, although fortunately avoiding the temptation to go over the top into potted meat sandwiches and fondant dainties. These occasions became renowned in certain circles and Siegfried, who couldn't resist literary references, always spoke of them as *soirées*. He liked to imagine himself presiding over them, dressed up as some nineteenth-century decadent, exchanging glittering conversation and wit with the guests and escaping his ennui for a couple of hours with alcohol and the occasional exotic *friandise*. However, Siegfried's and Janet's notions of these little parties were rather at odds with their actual style. They bore little resemblance either to informal civic functions or to *fin de siècle* literary *salons*. More often than not they were just an opportunity to exchange essential gossip, encouraged by an excess of drinking and interrupted only by the various comestibles which Janet had spent the whole afternoon preparing. The guests ranged from some of the campest (and, let's be honest, most vicious and unnecessarily shrill) people in London right through to dour political activists and benign heterosexual men (the kind you can kiss goodnight without having to make it into a big deal). In fact some of the activists and heterosexual men sometimes turned out to be the campest of all. In other words, most of the guests we had were to some extent queens irrespective of their sex and/or gender. Those biological or psychological men who pretend that, as though by some miracle or freak of nature, they don't have a queen screaming somewhere in their soul were the ones who weren't given a second invitation. The women and straight men who came were honorary queens, like Janet herself; and most accepted that honour with dignity and relish.

But don't get the idea that I'm into queens in a big way. Being camp and knowing that you are is only an achievement if that consciousness is parallel to the state of mind of someone like a saxophone player. Although being a queen is an existential attitude – it's charming, amusing, defiant and ultimately angry – the real dignity of not always taking your dick, yourself or other people as seriously as you're supposed to is as rare and as exciting as truth, the soulful side of pain.

It took Andy some time to accustom himself to it all. At first he would remain silent for most of the evening, deferentially observing Siegfried as he regaled the company with choice items of scandal, or quietly helping Janet with the food. He used to say he felt inadequate. Sometimes, when everyone had gone and we were clearing up, I'd come across scraps of paper covered with his doodles and fragments of writing. He always tried to snatch them away and if he succeeded he would destroy them as though he felt intolerably exposed by their content. I still have a few of them: eloquent comments on the more pretentious and bitchy aspects of the evening or sometimes disturbing evidence of his sense of isolation. I still find them humbling.

It took the sophisticates a while to adjust to the presence of Andy, too. His fear of their confidence was matched by their bewilderment at his sincerity. But eventually, and especially after he'd begun to invite his own guests, he became more self-assured and his intolerance of some of our more academically-minded acquaintances diminished: they started to accept each other or at least to accommodate for the duration of an evening certain cultural contradictions. Of course, Andy had to make more of an effort than anyone else despite all the lip-service to revolution, but I think he did provoke a genuine questioning, however slight, of some of the more outrageous assumptions of those present. Some of Siegfried's friends who often seemed incapable of expressing themselves in sentences which didn't contain foreign phrases or references to Donne actually began to speak English; there was a moderate raising of consciousness with regard to the practice of non-competitive conversation; people stopped feeling that it was necessary to be quite so blasé about French cheese and fresh lychees and began to admit that they enjoyed their food. Andy meanwhile developed a rather contrary taste for avocados, among other delicacies, and acquired almost overnight a working knowledge of parlari and Marxist-liberationist analysis and terminology.

The end of the *soirée* era coincided with Alex's holiday in Rome. When he came back, he found that Andy had moved to Hackney, leaving Janet somewhat at a loss (she would spend her evenings over a bit of sewing or watching TV). Uncle Siegfried was never there. He was always out at some pub or club, drinking. I didn't realise until later that he was cracking up.

In the Coleherne the butchest number I'd ever seen in my life bought me a drink. He'd come out of the Scrubs that day after serving two years for buggery. He mesmerised me. We went to the Masquerade and spent a while drinking with a nasty-looking copper. He and Butch were discussing firearms; Butch wanted to shoot the little queen who'd denounced him to the police. The irony didn't strike me at the time, and I observed it all as though it were the sort of thing that I came across every day. Outside, he dragged me into an alley and pushed my head down violently on his dick. It was unbelievably big. I could only get the tip in my mouth and even that nearly dislocated my jaw. Enraged, he pulled me back up and 'kissed' me. I thought he was going to rip my throat out. Then he bit my nose. The pain brought tears to my eyes.

'I'm going to shove this so far up your arse, you won't know what day it is,' he announced gruffly.

'It's too big,' I mumbled, aghast.

'You'll love it,' he assured me, 'everybody likes a bit of pain.'

My mind was beginning to fill with images of blood and screams. Trying not to panic I managed to convince him that we should go to my flat first. I said I didn't want to do it in the street. Drunkenly, he finally agreed. On the way (Where to? I kept wondering), he was lured into the all-night Wimpy, having caught sight of some jailbait he knew. We sat down with our coffee, talking about crime and punishment, even though the jailbait seemed a bit how's-your-father to me. I was desperate.

After a while I said I needed to make a phone-call to check if my (non-existent) flatmate was at home. The phone was by the door. I was out in a flash, haring down Earl's Court Road. I ran all the way to the British Airways terminal and just caught the nightbus as it was leaving. It was going in the wrong direction but I didn't care. I spent the rest of the night watching the porters in Covent Garden, feeling numb but alive. My visits to the Coleherne and to Earl's Court in general were terminated abruptly after that for several years, by which time I was unrecognisable. But these days the memory of it becomes less of a nightmare. His cock does go in.

It was at a party in Spandau that I met Guenther. We kissed and cuddled all night on someone's floor, surrounded by sleeping queens who had all had too much to drink to be interested in sex. He had blond hair and a matching moustache, but because he'd cultivated a rather child-like approach to me, I didn't suspect him of being butch. The night on the floor simply confirmed what I took to be a playful, role-refusing attitude on his part. I was surprised when I met him again: he took me straight upstairs to his flat, ripped my pants down, threw me on the bed and fucked me more brutally than he should have. He didn't seem to notice my discomfort, or perhaps he just didn't make a show of enjoying my pain. The transformation from soft boy into hard man – so improbable – is what I find so delectable about the memory.

Unexpected violence is no less of a problem than the more predictable kind. Who needs either? But both have a certain retrospective fascination.

There was no violence with Jonathan. He and I once visited Leighton House to investigate certain homoerotic artefacts. It was his idea. Lord Leighton, it should be remembered, lived only a few hundred yards from Holland Walk, which was where Jonathan had checked out my cock in the bushes, presumably to make sure that it was worth bothering to sacrifice his solitude before deciding whether to come home with me. He gave me some of his drugs before I fucked him. It was one of those drug-intense fucks which are really very self-centred, but which at the time seem to dissolve all bodily barriers like a Munch kiss.

We met often over the next few weeks. He shoved his dick up me one night somewhere in Westbourne Park and made one of his ironic comments. His eyes were sparkling with a sort of tender mockery of me and of himself. Perhaps it was the apparent equality of the relationship which made us both lose interest in it. I suppose we could have fallen in love instead. When I see him now we exchange telephone numbers, desultorily, each knowing that the other will never call.

That doesn't mean that I undervalue my remembrance of him. Perhaps, because of the circumstances, it took longer for him to become a regular jerk-off feature, but now he's one of the best. But an actual re-run would be a waste of time.

The most misleading element of this new diary is that it's still divided into conventional sequences of time: those dates which seem to have a reliable historical meaning. Clues to memory are dispersed there according to an historical order which is ultimately quite arbitrary in spite of the near-universal acceptance of its rationale. Siegfried predicted that I'd change it when it suited me like some Politburo historian. But are forgetting and remembrance questions of conscious effort?

These written fragments of the past may help to constitute a sense of the present, however illusory, but they're constantly at odds with the ahistorical workings of spontaneous memory and the interventions of forgetting. History poses as an objective critique of the anarchy of consciousness, while memory and desire, which are perhaps sometimes less anarchic than they seem, struggle with that crass account of reality to affirm some presence – a self. Unfortunately, the result isn't a sense of identity conveniently incorporated into the narrative of the world, it's more a vague sense of dislocation – loss, alienation, not-belonging, fragmentation, schizophrenia, despair, lack of faith: these are the words that some analyst may clutch at to fill the vacuum in his consulting parlour, to 'identify' that sense. But how pathetic it all is. I look at the diary as one may observe an 'accident' – a violent collision of experiences, breaching the walls of meaning. I look at it and I have to acknowledge its presence. Here it is, so to speak, a vestige of life, in which 'vestige' may represent that which has not been lost and 'life' may be taken as that which desires to survive.

These little ironies preserve me from myself. Just as the taste of another man's sperm, or the image of it, recalls me from that zone of involuntary exile which is hard to locate even in Siegfried's margin, but which is so familiar when you get there.

Halfway down the emergency stairs at the Angel tube station (that platform where you can be pushed onto the tracks from both sides) a young office-clerk sucked my dick. It hardly seems worth remembering, except that dick-sucking in public places is always edged with glamour because it's a crime.

There was more detail at Archway: I was in the middle cubicle. On one side was a boy of about sixteen with clear green eyes and a ragged T-shirt. On the other was a young man who looked distinctly anal-retentive, but handsome in a nazified way. All three of us were standing on the lavatory seats as though on plinths. The gap between the ceiling and the wall was wide enough for each to reach over and touch the next one's dick. I kissed the boy with green eyes – a deep lingering kiss, a bedroom kiss, while my hand gently played with a cock that was begging to be called boyish. (It was.) The boy came quickly – don't they always? – and left, but his eyes expressed more than sex. I wanted to rescue him from something. I turned to the cropped tough-guy next door. He was jerking himself off lovingly, worshipping his own dick, but needing other eyes as well. He allowed me to serve in the rites; I took over from him and soon his sperm came spurting out all over the place. He was just the type to have pints of fluid in him. We didn't kiss.

Somewhere in the East End a boy was jerking off, kneeling next to the wall. He wanted me to put my hand underneath and do it for him. On the other side of me was a young man, stark naked and very hairy. He was being jerked off by a person in the far-side cubicle. I put my hand through and pushed a finger up his furry arse. My mind was crazy with this image for hours afterwards but, really, what more did I want?

Sex-memories of London divide into two sections: pre- and post-European. It's not so much a territorial divide as one of attitude. In the former period my anonymity and my uninvolvement with the subculture made it possible for me to practise the schizoid life of the closet-queen with integrity, hardly noticing the contradictions which were the parameters of life then. Those memories are really the most accessible and fertile. The more recent ones are sometimes a little elusive. They haven't attained the iconic status of the others. Those that will endure are the ones which relate to experiences that were a kind of throwback to the earlier life, sexual acts which in themselves were more fantastic than substantial.

For over a year while Andy was here there was no new

input of material at all. And after he left, for a long time I remained celibate and grieving even during sex. Those incidents can never become sex-memories.

The acts and feelings which are reported in the diary are somehow less memorable than experiences which happened years ago and which were never written down. It's like the memory-tricks of senility. And during the passing of those years my youth itself has been transformed from experience into memory. I sometimes succeed in remembering myself then as an entity; more recent memories often merely confirm my present sense of incoherence.

Sometimes I shiver as I slide round these spirals. Perhaps you do, too. Or do you just jerk off to the music and laugh? This First World of ours is almost over, almost nothing more than a disk in the archive, but can you cope with that, you with the different memories but the similar eyes?

Part VIII

Siegfried was collecting sandbags on the quiet, in case of Armageddon. It wasn't the idea of individual death that worried him so much but he couldn't cope with the idea of Total Destruction. It stultified him, yet at the same time his mind hurried around trying to build its own shelter.

Andy's leaving may have been the last straw for Siegfried, but looking back on it, he was already reaching the end of his tether before any of that had happened.

'I'm beginning to see action itself as futile,' he moaned one afternoon when the conversation was taking a turn for the worse.

'Isn't that just what they want?' I suggested. 'Isn't that the best way of neutralising you? If you allow yourself to fall for their threats, you become literally hopeless. It's more important than ever before to refuse to accept that you're just some impotent individual. There has to be resistance. If you can't bring yourself to act collectively, you must at least resist at a personal level. Besides, it wouldn't harm you to go to a few meetings and demonstrations.' I knew it sounded a bit hollow. I felt nervous, and rather suprised at my own words, I, who observed the Labour Party with disdain, and who watched the news reports about Greenham Common as though it were all simply an episode in Coronation Street.

He was staring into his glass with black intensity. At length he spoke. His voice was remote, already quite isolated:

'This is the age of dog-mess. We've reached the point where the most heartfelt resistance has become virtually gratuitous. Technology isn't moved. We've reached the point where the "Horst Wessel Song" and the "Internationale", if sung often enough, will simultaneously bring tears to the eyes. The singing of "Rule Britannia" in the Vauxhall Tavern, which actually happens every week, is no longer absurd. The Nazi party's greatest strength was the disillusionment of those who had supported Social Democracy, who'd stopped seeing unfairness as a social ill and started taking it personally. But now it'll only take four minutes to transform everyone's front room into Auschwitz.' He paused for a moment and then almost snapped: 'Who said Japanese names were difficult to remember?' I didn't reply. 'Just look around you,' he continued, 'powerless people are still producing words and images, but the desperation that's behind them shows through. Like a growth. Just look at your diary.'

There was a long silence. I said nothing. Eventually he spoke again: 'The products of integrity, by which I mean those creative attempts on the life of reality which still have a point of departure in humanity, are either defeated by their own whimsy or they stand there helplessly like people shouting into the night. Their power was destroyed forty years ago. Their books have already been burnt and the systematic burning of the people has continued ever since. The War has never ended. A part of each of us was born at Nagasaki. It's not a question of them and us anymore; it's all internal now, too. The knowledge that human technology rather than God gives some people the power to decide when the day of judgement will occur – in which the judgement will naturally be authoritarian – makes individual commitment to a cause either an act of desperation or one of self-deception.'

'So where's the harm in resistance?' I asked. 'You've got nothing to lose, if what you say you feel is true.'

'I have no faith in the forms of resistance which are currently on offer,' he replied automatically, as if answering the question of a police interrogator for the hundredth time.

After a few moments, he looked up from his glass. His eyes seemed sadder and more vulnerable than usual.

'Perhaps you're right,' he said blankly.

That evening we went out together, to Clapham Common.

On the few occasions that he'd been there with me before he'd just hung around smoking and waiting for me to re-emerge from the shadows. That evening I must have been on the prowl only for about half an hour before I decided to forget it and go back to look for him. He wasn't in his usual place, so eventually I began to investigate the bushes again.

Not far away from the path I made out a group of people. When I approached I realised that one of them was Siegfried. He was lying face-down on the grass. Three men in leather were gang-banging him in silence.

Auntie Janet was watering her plants. She was lost in one of her pleasures. The pleasure is in watching them grow and flower; Janet appreciates that unexpected, gratuitous beauty – as though plainness and routine were not equally gratuitous. Squalor doesn't seem to surprise her. She can remember thinking when she worked in the factory that it was all quite inevitable. That whole human construct seemed more natural to her than the chance discovery of some commonplace little azure flower in an Alpine field – that was an enduring image from her one holiday, a trip to Switzerland to stay with some distant relatives. Yes, even Auntie Janet has distant relatives in Switzerland, though you wouldn't think it to look at her. She had sat in the field by the flower for a long time, feeling overwhelmed by something she could put no name to. She had wept without knowing why.

It saddens her if one of the plants ails or dies in winter, but in the end she accepts such things. Her attitude towards them is similar to her attitude towards people. Their destiny is an idea which is almost too tragic for her to tolerate; her only recourse is numb resignation, a moment of incredulity, before carrying on with whatever task she is engaged in.

Alex watched the careful irrigation work. After each dose of water, Janet would touch a leaf, put her nose to a flower, tamp down some soil . . . 'Does she never dream of being protected, worshipped, of surrendering herself completely to an ecstasy of irresponsibility?' He had to admit that it was unlikely. Janet was the kind who's been volunteering to do the washing-up since the age of six.

He thought of the photographs he'd seen of Janet with his grandparents. There were only three of them. In one picture his grandfather was holding her: a tiny child, her face hidden in the shawl, unrecognisable. The others were taken much later when she was already almost grown-up. There were several other people in these two pictures. It must have been a wedding or some special occasion. There was nothing in the composition of the images to suggest that any special relationship existed between her and his grandparents, nothing beyond some vague family resemblance, as of distant relatives. They were all just part of a group of people who were having their photograph taken.

Grace had been trying to persuade Janet to join the Labour Party. It was Grace who introduced her to the Women's Movement, too. At least you don't have to pay subs and have a renewable membership card for that. Janet's never been much of a card-carrying type: she doesn't really see the need to have credentials to authenticate either one's class-origins or one's commitment to social change. So despite Grace's urgings, she's more of an associate socialist than a party member, a supporter and reliable voter, the type of person who the party activists get a bit irritated by. But she's also just the sort of person they need; someone to help with the food at functions or to do the typing and stick the stamps on. Quite, thinks Janet.

I know what she means. Even in times such as these when the urge to stick leaflets through doors is often overwhelming, I'd still rather scrawl the slogans with my magic marker than align myself officially with the stripped pine and futon activists. And even if the party was still full of grass-roots homophobes with hearts of gold and no ambition, it wouldn't be any easier.

In other words, Janet and myself are the kind of unwilling heretics who come in for stick from the latter-day moralists. We may have to be shot one of these days in the interests of the revolution. That's assuming, of course, that we haven't been disposed of by the other side first. Janet says the Women's Movement isn't all it's cracked up to be, but she says she'd rather watch the burning of pornography in public, despite her doubts about such tactics, then have to watch the bureaucrats and bully-boys proclaiming soviets in which to tackle their ego-problems. Well, that's not what she says, but that's what it amounts to.

But, Siegfried, what about the barricades? 'The barricades which you seem to have in mind will not necessarily be the ones on which you have to take up a position.'

The trouble with Siegfried, and with me and Janet too if it comes to that, is that we live in a time when it's still possible to examine your doubts without actually starving to death or being gassed. Give us five years: if we haven't been blown up by then, we may at least have learned how to shoot straight. The trouble is that the shooting won't be coming from any of the sides we've been led to expect it of.

I didn't discover he was a soldier until after he'd fucked me. Perhaps this was fortunate. It meant that I avoided having to think in advance about the ethical implications of the act; by the time it was over I could invoke the spilled milk image. The fact that I needed this image is an indication of just how deeply one's political education can affect everyday activities however much one may rebel against it. Although I may tell myself that I'd have accepted his cock in any case – because I wanted to feel the thickness of it inside me, or because I wanted to spite my superego by taking forbidden fruit – I know that either I'd never have managed it or the whole thing would have been ruined by guilt. Think of the rough trade from Sheffield whose cock I certainly wanted but whom I rebuffed when he uttered the word 'bhindi' without a trace of self-consciousness. The desire for cock and the opportunity to make a memory were both put quite firmly in their place. So is it just a game to trick myself if I avoid pre-sexual fact-finding talk? Not rebellion at all, but a cheap excuse that justifies anything? Soldiers kill Irish people and Argentinians. Who needs their cocks or their uniforms? Perhaps Mr Muswell Hill does. He's a middle-class boy with all the appropriate fantasies. He got a hard-on when I told him about the time that Andy and I were attacked by Cup

Final fans. Perhaps he was the person who wrote on the pisshouse wall: 'Skinheads are the only real men. Piss on me while I lick your boots' . . . Parents, teachers and macho fools leave scars as big as bullet-holes in our minds.

What about those bhindis, anyway? History doesn't permit us the simple pleasures of straightforward interethnic fucking: power intervenes. In this discourse there is the master and the slave, the dinge-queen and the snow-queen and beyond them there is the cool nigger who screws honkies. Also, on the other side, there are those dubious idealists who manage to convince themselves and perhaps each other that they really are just having a fuck that's beyond reproach from whatever quarter; the white ones in their lonely hearts adverts have 'Caribbean interests'. Oh yeah. And are the black ones doing it because they think that all white men have horsedicks, natural rhythm and sensual lips?

But non-procreative miscegenation is all the rage these days. The hottest videos feature black dicks as big as cucumbers and white cops in riot gear with nightsticks ready-greased. It turns people on in spite of the machine-gun, so they say. Jefferson, somehow shouting louder than the shouts of his own slaves said, *We hold these truths to be self-evident, that all men are created equal*; and a while later Gandhi added, somewhat inscrutably, *Truth ever is, untruth never was.* On the wall of a squat in Brixton (demolished after some civil disturbance in that area) someone had daubed a quote from a song called 'Blues for Mama': *Ain't nobody perfect, cause ain't nobody free.* It's all good, but it's not good enough. The crack of rhino-whips still drums other words into our minds, breaking hearts and limbs and adding old meanings to new images . . . (Perhaps if you're black, you didn't assume that Ivan was white. Did you? 'Colour unimportant' say the honky lonely hearts. Nigger-lover. Uncle Tom. Whore of Babylon.)

That image of the black child and the white child together, neither aware of their own destiny, is just a polaroid print that will curl up and crumble in the flames.

Everyone is different, but no-one is equal yet, no-one is

free . . . remember that, black man, white man, the next time one of you is saying *kiss-my-ass* to the other with that innocent look on your face.

Paul might be a snow-queen, but he's young and beautiful and a perfect one to remember, not least for his refusal to be either queen or stud: he's both in a way, but never oppressively or self-oppressively. I worry about his interest in drugs, although perhaps he knows what he's doing.

There's a faint, sweet smell about him, even after sex, when his hand searches for mine and I feel his lips still wanting diaphanous kisses. His revolutionary smile, which I can feel even when I can't see it, is what I will remember best. It reminds me that at least one per cent isn't shit.

It doesn't seem to help Siegfried to be any less metaphysical when he claims that metaphysical despair is a First World luxury, but then why should it? Beyond the parks and commons, in the squalor of the council estates, metaphysics is no stranger, no luxury: it's in the sex-manuals which are hidden under the bed, and in the bruises of battered women. In this world only meanings are a luxury. Someone is finally collapsing into tears while the rest of the family is sitting at the dinner-table, looking on in mystified horror.

You speak of vulnerability and abandonment, but don't you feel the shudder of the centuries as you speak? They are undeliverable cargoes. And don't you feel the seat vibrate with the laughter of insomniacs? Is it just weariness and hysteria or are whole ages shaking with laughter while inwardly they shiver with fever and fatigue? Aren't you shivering? I watch the grotesques and the phonies in the bars, trying to remind myself that they were not always grotesque, making the effort to analyse the tragedy of their phoneyness. Faces lit by pinball machines have eyes that seem gluttonous, like the eyes of famine or prison . . .

Nothing is too extreme now. Despair makes everything seem like freedom.

The drag-artistes are mass-murderers.

The videos show snuff-films.

Cocksuckings and fistfuckings LIVE ON STAGE!

'I'll have breasts before I get of here,' said the male-to-female TS, but what's so outrageous about that?

Shove EVERYTHING up my arse, *this* is liberation.

Outside is the Depression and, yes, some kind of Fascism is quite fasionable in this season's evening-wear collections. A decadent, exciting look for the modern world.

'Choke me with your dick, nigger. Wham it right up. Who cares, we'll all be bombed next year.'

The real straight boys are joining up one way or the other; *so* butch. What? The note under the wall says 'Can I fuck you, yes or no?' Forget the acquired immune deficiency syndrome, just bend over, cunt.

He's jerking off and my eye is pressed to the hole, watching, like anyone would. I can see the spunk dripping onto the hairs on his leg and I've got a hard-on.

Remember that policeman at Heaven who wanted to suck you off? He's probably got a mortgage. The car-workers all have mortgages these days.

A leatherman couldn't wait to get his finger, his tongue, his dick into my arse. The poppers did the trick. Then he withdrew and jerked off.

Where does desire come into this? In the Parc des Buttes-Chaumont a man pushed two fingers up my arse and I did desire that. I desire to keep the memory unrepressed. Sometimes I will try to be at one with that image, all these irresponsible images, even though none of it is quite real except when words and memories converge for a few moments of immortality. I mean for a few moments of respite from the material world, in which all experiences are rehearsals for death and where I am excluded from my own actions like a murderer who only watched himself clubbing the brains out of his victim's head.

But no, it's not that easy. My responsibiity isn't diminished. I'm not a Nazi claiming that I only acted under orders. My exclusion is illusory – at least on the good days, when the kisses don't curdle in my mouth and I manage not to lose my sense of humour.

Part IX

Not suprisingly, perhaps, the roles which Andy and Alex adopted while they were together remained contradictory and blurred. It would be crude to try and clarify their positions in conventional terms and also rather complicated, besides probably being a bit of a bore for everyone else. At times they would both have passed the test as sadists, at others they made distinguished and valiant efforts at masochism. The in-between combinations were possibly the most forthcoming. But it's really quite inappropriate to discuss the matter with reference to their sexual behaviour – although, of course, some prurient and indelicate mind-boggler would have a field day analysing all that. It's more a question for me of trying to do justice to the affection that existed between them (where matters of power often cease to be so important) and of appraising the ambiguity of how it was or wasn't expressed.

What so disarmed me when I first met him was his ingenuousness. It was terrifying to see such vulnerability. There was also a perverse urge to abuse it: like seeing someone on a ledge and feeling that you can choose whether to pull (him) to safety or push (him) off.

The years of self-imposed emotional solitude had left Alex with certain dubious advantages, one of the more obvious being that he was never visibly out on that ledge. At the same time he dreamed of being seen there, risking everything, giving someone that awful choice of rescue or murder. In a world of more than one person, it isn't ever a question of suicide, even if you jump.

Andy was on the ledge and he wanted to get off. Our time together was a period in which we tried to effect a very complex manoeuvre: I tried to pull him to safety while also climbing out there and expecting him to do the same for me. It was in that bizarre contortion that we found some moments of true, reciprocal affection, each of us holding the other unselfishly, each acknowledging the other's exposed life and being able to accept the responsibility of protecting it. Not very often, of course: among those moments were all the others – the destructive, uncaring moments when one feels compelled to exploit someone else's weakness in order to give oneself an illusion of strength; and the moments of self-indulgent, self-pitying meanness when one encourages that exploitation in order to feel one's sense of being hard-done-by confirmed and consolidated.

Perhaps sadomasochism is a game of rescue and murder enacted on a non-existent ledge, removed, like all games, from the dangers of life, playing safely with the idea of those dangers. But perhaps that removal also distances the players too far from life itself. The real exposure of one's vulnerability is different from letting someone's cigarette loose on your nipples.

Affection is a mutual yielding, a tenderness, and at the same time it requires strength, expressed not in handcuffs and whips but in the power of being able to be responsible for yourself and for another person. Respect. Perhaps it only emerges briefly in those tenuous and inevitably ephemeral relationships like mine and Andy's. Life is so difficult to deal with except in small doses. The rest, which for safety's sake is defined by the rules of some game, is perhaps ultimately a question of abuse, parody, refusal and cheating. All that crap about winners and losers.

Andy is the only one who ever let me crawl out beside him. He is the only one who ever pulled me back and let me believe for a while that I wasn't alone. Who could forget that?

But it's a memory that'll never be sentimental. He didn't orphan me. It will just endure, passionately and with rather more sensuousness than the memories of him which aren't so uplifting, the ones that remind of how it's really quite a relief that it's over now.

There's no Mr Right, Janet. And who wants a Mr

Compromise? Settle down to what?

A long time ago Andy put his forehead on my shoulder in a gesture of complete trust among all the other gestures of defiance, of resentment and of unhappiness. I touched his head. The hair was cropped; it felt like mink. I was physically overwhelmed. His small perfect ear was against my lips, waiting for a kiss. I nudged it with my tongue, wanting to protect him, but pulled away abruptly, protecting myself instead. His animal ears, his wide, sad eyes, his wet tongue. Our times of belief in each other were so short-lived.

By the time Andy was ready to move out, he had already acquired the habit of going to Cha-Cha without me. This was around the period of Cha-Cha's golden age, when only those in the know were there and when Scarlett would perch like a mediaeval anti-pope in the lobby, gratuitously refusing entry to those unfortunates who happened to displease her eye. She would extend her hand to those who were permitted to pass the cash desk as though to receive a devout kiss. In fact, all she wanted was to stamp the back of your hand with an indelible mark so that you could use the one-way valve into Heaven without fear of remaining trapped on the wrong side of the doors. She was usually surrounded by a group of sycophants who would eye the potential nightclubbers with a mixture of contempt and gluttony; only Scarlett herself, the boddhisattva of the shrine, had perfected the technique of total impassivity, perhaps occasionally allowing an almost imperceptible smile to haunt her face for an instant in acknowledgement of some particularly gratifying arrival.

Past Scarlett, in the magical interior, despair was already running riot: vodkas were tossed back frantically, the flow being halted only by the obligation to return the mindless greetings of those who had just entered; the speed was beginning to take effect; the ritual promenading was underway, like a scene from the court at Versailles. Siegfried should have known better than to come here on his own. It was asking for trouble. I think trouble was just what he wanted, though. And what better place to stage the first public performance of one's death than here, where the cheapness of the emotion was rivalled only by the insincerity which engendered it. He needed to follow through the logic of himself to the point where he disintegrated. Cha-Cha, the palace of trash, was ideal.

We were all there, naturally, but the fact that Siegfried had arrived on his own seemed to compel him to pretend that we weren't. He was drinking heavily, though perhaps not quite so heavily as Andy who was already in a trance despite being more than aware that Siegfried had invaded his territory. What really seemed to cook Siegfried's goose was that Andy didn't even appear to recognise him: they kept passing on the stairs and each time Andy's eyes would glaze over as though he were encountering not an intimate but a piece of garbage, the very sight of which was so offensive that he needed to tell himself it didn't exist.

Siegfried couldn't have appreciated at this point why Andy had to behave like this or why it was that he, Siegfried, was exploring the possibilities of personal disintegration with such zeal. But somehow he managed not to go to pieces immediately; in the same way that people will spend three hours in a club before actually engaging with the task of securing a sex-partner (it's to do with a respect for dramatic principles) Siegfried seemed to know that he must wait until at least half-past two before allowing his heart to break.

Meanwhile he and Andy were rushing back and forth between the spheres of Heaven and Cha-Cha, between each of these chambers which in their own way were both vibrating with anger, fear and anguish. The edges of Siegfried's perceptions were beginning to bleed, like the images on inferior video-tape; whole areas were fading into brownish stains, leaving only those words 'I love you' – uttered at last, and almost to his own surprise – to form in necessary, essential isolation somewhere within his smudged consciousness. Andy and Claire were dancing. Norma and Thomas were talking to Pas and the others. Siegfried's nerves were swirling together, mustering for the attack. He was preparing for an act of faith which he sensed in advance to be doomed.

Somehow he got from the bar to the dance floor without collapsing. He tugged at Andy's shirt, a garment which suddenly seemed to him very beautiful: 'I want to say that I love you. I might not get another chance.' Then out, pushing through the crowd (who are used to histrionics – just another queen freaking out) and into Hungerford Lane, feeling how odd it is that all these images will never be repeated. Siegfried reached the night bus in record time. He was thus denied the *frisson* of actually seeing Norma running through Trafalgar Square in her Quattrocento Palio outfit in pursuit of him; he was denied the thrill of seeing Thomas cruising up and down the Embankment in search of a figure poised on the bridge or, perhaps, of ripples rising to the surface; he was denied the look on Andy's face as he returned abruptly to sobriety, his face which in the process recaptured all the youth that a night at Cha-Cha had claimed.

When Andy got home, he discovered that Siegfried had already had time to write a little note before passing out on the bathroom floor with a knife in his hand. No veins had been opened although this did not mean that no death had occurred. The rest of the household was still, unaware of anything.

Siegfried awoke in bed. Andy was offering him coffee and cigarettes, the first aid of the desperate. Then came the tears: it was the equivalent in this deathbed scene of the relaxation of the bowels, but it was also the first manifestation of grief to trickle into the changed world. Siegfried was weeping for his own passing which had now begun. And he was weeping for Andy and Alex who were about to discover that sooner or later liberation always brings with it an inconsolable yearning for the bondage it has destroyed. Andy slept in an adjacent room that night and Siegfried was left hunched beneath the bookshelves which rose about his head. 'Look what I'm reduced to,' he murmured, unaware of echoing the words of Auntie Janet, who used them often but, happily, in a rather different context. He looked at the books wrily and smiled. A multitude of ironies which only he appreciated seemed to be contained within their covers. Then he slept, in preparation for the remainder of his death, which even he could not have imagined to be so protracted nor so painfully necessary.

Perhaps one of the ironies which had twitched a smile out of Siegfried's grim lips was the presence on the shelves of a modern translation of the *Phaedrus*. To one whose interest in the art of rhetoric and whose addiction to the use of dialogue was outstripped only now by a desire to memorise his and his beloved's all but allegorical journey through soul and body, the final remark of Phaedrus – '. . . Socrates, friends should share everything' – may have hovered deliciously at the edge of his mind, waiting like a trusting dog for his pat on the head, but getting only that last, uncompromisingly Socratic rejoinder: 'Let us be going.'

Siegfried may or may not have been dying, but his ghost was already haunting me. This breakdown, in which he disintegrated physically and morally, in no way released me from the burden of having to listen to him.

'People see me as a foolish libertarian,' said the ghost, who was lying in bed, looking miserable. Next to him, on the night-table, was a copy of a book to which Siegfried had contributed. It was a collection of essays in which various persons declared their attitude towards anarchism. Siegfried's piece had been a short panegyric on heresy. I remember how hurt he had been when the book first appeared: Andy had made some disparaging remark, completely dismissing the event – failing to realise that Siegfried, too, was occasionally in need of experiencing a moment of glory, no matter how illusory.

The ghost lay there quietly for a few moments, as if collecting his thoughts. Just as he was about to speak, Janet brought the tea in. The tea, perhaps not surprisingly, was lapsang souchong.

'It's lapsang,' said Janet, unnecessarily. We both looked at her with mild amusement, but she didn't twig. However, she did realise that the situation no longer required her presence, and left, tactfully closing the door behind her.

The ghost took sugar. I poured two cups and sweetened one of them for him. 'Your uncle Siegfried,' he said, 'always took life rather seriously. His occasional moments of levity were usually short-lived and near-hysterical – a drunken prelude to despair. His *Weltschmertz* was as chronic as his drinking, and he submitted to it with an almost sensual abandon, in the best Jewish-humanitarian tradition. Who else but cosmopolitan Jewish intellectuals burst into tears at news reports of popular uprisings or authoritarian counter-moves? His unwilling misanthropy, his fatalism and negativity, and his moments of sublime elation were all peculiarly overstated and rather melodramatic – a bit like his death. You see, he didn't fit in well to the English spiritual climate, which is one where fanaticism and cynicism circumscribe a huge sphere of pettifogging complacency and cheerful small-mindedness. He couldn't relate very easily to the mediocrity of everyday life, and when he did, it was generally more in empathy with the suffering that mediocrity conceals than in some patronising gesture of solidarity. He embodied certain tragic aspects of the human spirit, and almost inevitably, he experienced this as despair. Despair was his cultural inheritance.'

I would have made some contribution here, but the ghost was clearly unprepared for interruptions. He was scrutinising a passport-size photograph of Andy which had been glued to the bottom of the bookshelves.

He pursued his subject: 'His way of coping with it all was that rather patriarchal, domineering attitude. It preserved him – most of the time, anyway – from simply breaking down into a deluge of tears. He used to shout at Andy just so that he wouldn't end up whimpering in complete abjection at what he perceived as his inability to communicate with anyone. Andy did have some intuition of this, but it didn't make it any easier for him to live with Siegfried. The actual incidents which caused the rows were all totally insignificant of course: a towel not folded properly on the rail; knives and forks left in the washing-up bowl when Andy did the dishes; Andy's extravagances – you remember how it was when Siegfried felt that one of Andy's purchases was not a "household essential". But even Siegfried realised that it wasn't these manifestations of Andy's anarchic side which were the root of the problem. The problem was the relationship itself: he just couldn't allow you and Andy to get away with any illusions. You had to be as aware as he of the flaws – the underlying tragedy of any attempt at overcoming one's personal emotional isolation. He wanted perfection and harmony, and because it wasn't there (as if it ever could be . . .), he constructed for you an epic of failure and discord. It confirmed his awful perception of the squalor of existence. And whenever Andy and you managed to keep that squalor at bay, you notice that Siegfried mysteriously disappeared, as though unable to contemplate the very experiences which he most dreamed of.'

I kept wondering whether this was an epitaph or the song of the Phoenix. Either way, it didn't matter – the ghost was pausing only long enough to gulp his tea. (At least, it wasn't alcoholic.) 'You'll be aware, of course, that Siegfried's fondness for Andy was extreme. Andy was the only person who had ever treated him with that mixture of respect and contempt which surpasses mere admiration or dismissiveness. Siegfried never quite got over it – he'd been too used to being treated either as an extraordinary creature or as an insect. Andy's refusal to treat him as anything other than a human being flummoxed him. That's why he always seemed to be feeling a bit awkward while Andy was around. Unfortunately, he ended up with two images of Andy which he could never quite reconcile: one which he adored, as though Andy were his own delightful son; and the other, which consistently reminded him that Andy was an independent person, full of the usual contradictions, whose life could be as remote from Siegfried as that of anyone else. That conflict was, in my opinion, one of the major factors in convincing Andy that he must leave. Why after all should he have had to put up with the classically ambiguous role thus assigned to him? Siegfried, who couldn't resolve the conflict within himself, had chosen Andy as a victim for his experiments in ethics. But even Andy, whose victim-trip may appear to some to be well under way, was unwilling to be a voodoo doll.'

It wasn't that I resented the remarks that the ghost was making. I was just finding it difficult to adjust to the idea of his making remarks in the first place. For a start, Siegfried was still clinically alive.

'Would you like another cup?' I asked.

'No thanks,' he replied, 'I'm a bit tired. I think I'll try to sleep for a while.'

I left him there, staring at the photograph.

Part X

Alex was in the great wilderness of Heaven, inspecting his moustache in the mirror and simultaneously appraising the beasts as they roamed in herds in and out of the lavatory. He wasn't exactly desperate but not quite at peace enough with himself to be able to leave without having deposited some visible reminder of his desire in his wake. A small South Asian rockabilly smiled affably and politely invited him to share a cubicle in the Ladies.

Some remnant of Islam must have been troubling this boy: kisses were reserved only for the neck and Alex's cock may as well not have been there.

'Do you like being screwed?' asked the boy, ever polite.

'Yes,' said Alex, not wanting to beat about the bush too much in a situation which clearly didn't have any potential for the questioning of roles.

The boy fucked him quite proficiently, but rather unremarkably. What stuck in his mind afterwards as he was doing a quick jerk-off replay at home in bed, was the furry feeling of the boy's hair. It had been like getting fucked by a small mammal, the sort that the Council permits one to keep in cages on large housing-estates.

Alex rarely meets sex-partners at parties, at least not straight-identified and uninvited men. But it did happen once. The man kept looking at him all evening. 'Ambiguous' would inevitably be the word to describe that look. Alex was intrigued, naturally, not least by the ritual knife-scars on the man's cheek.

Eventually he offered me a lift home and I took him into the bedroom. His courage seemed to be failing him, so I unzipped his fly and sucked an erection out of him. He didn't protest, but after a few minutes he said he ought to be going. I carried on, relentlessly. Then, rather hysterically I thought, he pulled my trousers down and fucked me, not violently but not very tenderly. It all seemed to be a bit of a problem for him, poor thing. He stopped before orgasm and began to ask me about one of the women at the party. There are limits to my generosity with regard to the neuroses of 'straight' men, so I showed him to the door and suggested that he go back and look for her. It was only then, on my own, that I could really begin to appreciate the feel of his cock.

Siegfried predicted that I'd change my past in order to suit what I thought might be an interesting present. But the process of changing history is rather remote from that of trying to perceive through apparently arbitrary fragments of the past some hint of what may constitute a presence. The philosophical problems of distinguishing what may be the past from what may be the present are no less daunting than the psychoanalytical ones and both have some bearing on history.

If I call my diary a 'yearbook' does that mean that it ceases to resemble the process of repression? As a document it's authentic enough. However, my fecal matter is an equally authentic product of my digestive processes but it's still despised by most other people irrespective of its value as documentary (or other) evidence. So if I call my diary a 'digest', does that help? Nothing helps if I shall always have these memories to dwell on between now and death. The only escape would be if it were possible again, however fleetingly, to find a way into the present which doesn't remind me of any past.

Personal past, I mean. I don't want some dream-sequence which denies this nasty world and its nasty history. You and I, down at Greenwich in the sunset, let us always remember how heartbreaking the world is. Let us not forget that this violent collision of light and city is a brutalist artefact which may appeal to our taste for the unwonted but which is in fact an inevitable image of death. It's the image of the police-computer VDU; it's the image of the hard-ons and the orgasms which soldiers get when they pull the trigger; it's the image of a queerbashed skull thudding on concrete, or of a woman whose husband gets a bit out of order when he's had a couple of drinks; it's the image of the bruises that don't show up on a black boy's body after he's spent the night in custody. The bigger the warhead, the more violent the collision of light and city. The redder the sky. The greyer the river.

The city . . . a myth?

Siegfried wasn't dead in the conventional sense, OK, but from now on it was only ever his ghost who spoke to us. After his struggle with philosophy on the bathroom floor, he began the long process of removing himself from those areas of life where, despite everything, he had previously managed to give the impression of being socially useful. Almost every day they would phone Janet from Siegfried's place of work, asking where he was. She was never certain, but she had her suspicions. The ghost finally told her what was going on: Siegfried would go into work as usual, but by eleven o'clock his mind would begin to wander. Andy, I love you. And he'd start to feel the cramps in his stomach. So he'd go downstairs quietly and slip out when no-one was looking. Then he'd walk over the common – it was late spring – and watch the activity. Some schoolkids who had bunked off would be sniffing glue under the bandstand; babies under escort would be playing on the grass and shitting themselves without a care; retired people would be sitting on benches or standing, seemingly in awe of the world, as though they had never actually seen it properly before; and there would be the occasional unemployed faggot killing time, nonchalantly cruising or perhaps, for once, just getting some fresh air. All this calmed Siegfried. It gave him some perspective on things, reminding him that his own disintegration actually deprived the world of very little. That feeling of insignificance was reassuring; it curbed for a while his feeling that it was the world rather than he that was disintegrating. He'd spend perhaps two hours quietly observing these goings-on and then would return to work where he would do virtually nothing until five o'clock. They were very sympathetic at work, but they couldn't afford to employ someone who wasn't doing his job, so they suggested a break. Siegfried took a fortnight off. He knew that it wouldn't make any difference and so did his employers. When he came back they put it to him tactfully that perhaps he should be thinking of alternative employment. Siegfried, who had never been a one to need telling twice in this kind of situation, received his leaving present politely. He was still self-possessed enough, in private, to find it all rather amusing. It was like being sent off to an old people's home by one's concerned but nonetheless impatient family.

It was thus that Siegfried was left uninterrupted during the day, with the exception of a monthly trip to the Unemployment Benefit Office, to muse on the problems of faith and tragedy and to keep on breaking his heart in the hope of eventually anaesthetising it. His ghost pottered around the house moodily, getting on everyone's nerves and under Janet's feet. But we put up with it. After all, we knew what it was like.

One evening I was at home, minding my own business. Siegfried's ghost was lounging around, bored.

'You're a child, Alex,' he said abruptly. He seemed to have been at the drink again. 'You're none the worse for that, but like a child, your experience of life vacillates between pleasure and pain as though there were no intermediary stages. One minute you're blissfully fucking with someone you don't even know and the next you're in tears at what a terrible mess you and the rest of humanity are in.'

Siegfried could get away with a lot – I was prepared to put up with most of it without protest, but I wasn't going to put up with as much from his fucking ghost.

'Listen,' I said, leaning against a chair so that he wouldn't notice I was shaking, 'you sit there getting pissed on booze that Janet has bought you out of her Giro, pontificating on whatever subject happens to cross your self-obsessed brain or moping around the house doing fuck-all and expecting everybody else to look after you, and then you have the nerve to patronise *me* as though you, yourself, were somehow miraculously able to transcend your own conflicts and have a dispassionate and sagacious insight into somebody else's life. Well, fuck off, bitch. What I've learned on the streets is just as valid as what you've managed to steal from books . . .' I trailed off, unsure of which direction to take. The ghost looked a bit taken aback and for a moment he just eyed me silently. Then he smiled. I realised that I'd lit a second cigarette without finishing the first.

'That merely confirms what I was just saying,' he said smugly. He was fiddling idly (or so it seemed) with a small metal brooch which he'd recently taken to wearing on his lapel. 'You know as well as I that Siegfried's acquaintance with the life of the streets – or the parks, if it comes to that – was just as thorough as yours is. The difference is that Siegfried perceived that the external aspects of life are no more or less important than the internal ones. His perception obviously influences my own approach . . . '

'What you're really saying,' I interrupted, 'is that a pseudo-Zen monk who occasionally goes to the brothel is better qualified to cope with himself and with the world than I am. It wouldn't do for you at all to recognise that at times those "external aspects of life" become so dominant that they have to be given some kind of priority. Try slashing your wrists again and see what your approach is then.' He didn't like that. 'I wouldn't mind so much,' I went on, almost shouting. I felt as though a line of speed had just hit me. 'I wouldn't mind if all I ever did was have mindless sex, whether or not with strangers, or spent my whole time plotting the overthrow of the state; I wouldn't mind if *you* had some legitimate claim to living a life where the personal and the political coincided – which is probably the nearest anybody will ever get to some form of Zen – but you don't: you just sit there with catatonic anxiety, grumbling and criticising and being superbly detached in some convenient corner of Siegfried's invulnerable margin. And then you turn round and attack me because it *disturbs* you to see somebody who doesn't resort to philosophical get-out clauses in times of conflict and who still manages to keep going. That's the real problem.' In spite of myself, I noticed the Renoir picture. She was still being enchanted by Puccini. 'You don't *want* to believe in that non-abstract approach. But if you don't believe it, it's like saying that you don't believe detainees could still fall in love with each other in the concentration camps. Find me some "intermediary stages" between the pleasure and pain of that!'

The ghost had pretended to fall asleep. I was tempted to smack him, but decided I probably didn't need to. He didn't speak to me again for two days.

In spite of his annoyance at me, Siegfried's ghost couldn't resist shooting his mouth off. He was in the Two Brewers when I walked in. We glared at each other from opposite sides of the dance floor for about an hour. Eventually I couldn't bear it any longer and went over to speak to him.

'I don't know why you should be so surprised. Is your presence here any more appropriate than mine?'

'Appropriate to what?' I asked.

Siegfried's ghost raised his eyebrow very slightly and gulped down some beer (he was trying to look down-to-earth). I felt that he was drinking now only so as to avoid smirking. Of course, he didn't answer my question.

'The thing about rough trade,' he said, as if that was what we had just been discussing, 'the thing that seems so attractive, is the absence of a veneer of respectability. I mean respectability in the sense of that polite awkwardness about the physical and the sexual which is never quite overcome even in the most "uninhibited" middle-class situations.' Siegfried's ghost was the type who didn't like having to fart in front of the person who'd just fucked him. 'Don't you find that even a person's good looks can lose their sexual attractiveness if you find that person to be *over*-cultivated?'

'I'm not quite sure what you mean,' I replied, honestly.

'Well, a simplified example would be that of a middle-class faggot who was exclusively attracted to, say, white working-class or black men. His classism and racism would lead him to believe that these categories of people were somehow closer to their sexual selves than the middle-class men whose culture he had actually experienced and perhaps understood. This person imagines that middle-class people are too "cultivated" to be able to have "uninhibited" sex – by which he means the kind of sex which is, in his culture, morally unacceptable, but which he, nevertheless, desires. Being, himself, a morally unacceptable creature, he sees no conflict between experiencing these desires and being middle-class because his moral position has made it possible for him to avoid the scruples which inhibit others. He's not stupid enough to imagine that he is the only middle-class person in this position – logically, he has to recognise that many other faggots, for instance, will similarly have access to their forbidden desires – but at a symbolic level, he is alone. People from a different background, also at a symbolic level, represent the free flow of desire . . . '

'But you could look at it from a different perspective,' I said, almost interrupting him. He looked at me rather acidly. 'You could say that we're all mad, but that we live our madness differently, so that our desires appear to be diverse, determined by class, power or whatever. But perhaps it's just that queens live their madness and get punished most severely for it even by other gay men, while politicals rationalise the situation – as though they weren't mad at all – and butch queens just repress it so thoroughly that they convince themselves that they're actually normal. Of course, they only fool themselves.'

Siegfried's ghost seemed to be thinking over this point and was just about to make some clever reply to it when the bell for last orders rang. He finished his drink in a panic and immediately rushed to the bar. I was only now beginning to understand that he was just a ghost, a rather irritating but sometimes comforting remnant of a period of life that was past. I watched him for a few moments as he pushed his way forward at the bar. He could have been anybody. I went out, leaving him to his grave.

The Paean

His grave; my excavations.

There are still fuck knows how many of these dialogues. The cemeteries are full of them. In time they become less audible but never quite silent. In space they shrink out of sight, but like the invisible question-marks hovering at the end of apparent statements, these dialogues are always with us.

The memories are even more untellable than the dialogues. That straight man at the party was perhaps one of the least, but certainly not the last. The perfection of the empty page, the diary with no entries, is quite beyond reach. And even if my words may eventually give way to the lines which represent Andy's fantasms, the images of cock and arse and spurting semen are endlessly the same. There's no nirvana. At least, not until you stop trying to believe in one, not until romance and sex abandon the turpitude you have consigned them to in your desperate ignorance. You and I, poor souls, not even really knowing the depth of our faith, we hibernate among frayed leaves and among the shadows of this moral winter, waiting stupidly for death. I say "you and I", and I hardly know who I mean because the phrase so overwhelms me with tenderness and loathing, my naked politics. Perhaps you say "I and I" and clothe your faith in the soft brown eyes of Africa, where identity is no longer the difference between you and me. Soul. Or maybe you take too much speed and whir along ahead beyond all this fancy stuff, a cool third person, very singular, and almost at one with no-one. The size-queens gasp at us all in disbelief as they grease up their massive dildoes and search yet again for the superlative – truth, beauty, the angel of death. Is that all ye know on earth?

And all I can offer is interruption, in a temporary escape from these words because there are enough of them now. Completion, perfection, 'The End', all these idiotic substitutes for saying *enough*, are always just interruptions in disguise. There's no end here, just as there was no beginning. And it's no more of a mess than most things. But who can resist providing some sort of epitaph? It's one of the more delicious imperatives of death.

For Alex and Andy friendship can never be *enough*, just as their love-affairs will always fail to convince them that they are not alone. But each will find in the other's respect and enduring loyalty an image of the antidote to tragedy. Only an image, perhaps, but worth the search, the passionate search which is still too much of a beginning for it to be an agony. Love, like brotherhood, is for life.

Siegfried and Janet have survived efforts to reintegrate them into an intelligible design. Their voices echo in my ears like those of angels or demons.

Siegfried, this zombie of the modern world, lives where he is needed, even if only in the form of a ghost. His vague personality is still an unmistakable presence; his shattered identity is still strong enough to be given official recognition. He's taken more than his fair share of my energy, but I respect him even if only because he's never resorted to malice as an easy option. Paradox and irony apart, it is he who will accompany my coffin.

My fondness for Janet needs little further comment. She is my aunt by courtesy of the imagination of the leper-queens. Being more sensitive to the immanence of tragedy than their butch brothers, they've recognised the value of mockery and in particular self-mockery. Janet's dignity is parallel to their sense of absurdity. The two are always parallel and mutually supportive, perhaps even interdependent. She continues to be a point of spiritual reference in my life, this occasionally dignified life in a largely absurd world. She will die obscurely and alone, but not unremembered.

A last word for myself: 'he and I were almost one' –

almost, but never quite. And here I am, alone with memories of sex and men's dicks and Andy, memories of the times I've tried not to be alone and of the times I've tried to reach images of myself in these fluttering worlds which fall but never settle, like city snow. Alone with all those unresolved questions, words and images which might have sparkled a hundred years ago, but now seem so insubstantial, so out of place in a life which can be felt more powerfully through the rectum: the thicker the cock, the more powerful the pulsations of somebody else's loneliness, the blood and sperm of their incommunicable solitude.

Myself and my diary: words rescued from utter sadness by an even more painful irony which deceptively indicates me as an individual, one of those innumerable would-be flowers. There's no coming to terms with it. But I can acknowledge the fragmentation, the becoming and the ceasing to be, the never-achieved but still desired integrity . . . Forgive me if I'm left with memories of people where there was only the time and the space for the rapid release of our spunk – memorable gifts, the existence of which may have allowed us momentarily to feel more deeply *our* existence; and the emptiness after the release . . .

An emptiness in which humanity somehow demands my respect and my generosity (the most mysterious and beautiful of *anybody's* features). That humanity is not pretty; it's the faceless and the miserable, the abused, the humiliated, the injured, the brutalised, the starving, the degraded, the persecuted, the dead. I am so remote from them that I feel mystified by my concern for them. It's perhaps precisely not *my* concern, but a collective dread which rushes into the emptiness at those times when I'm least self-possessed, when I'm abandoned even by the shadows of my desire to possess my self or another – this space and time between being and having . . . these multitudes, ourselves. What more can I say? I love you? That's what the Franciscans would say, even while the Fascists were tearing off their knee-caps. Well, no, I don't love that knee-capping part of you, however bad your life may have been. And I don't love that part of you which is cheap and insincere, the part of you that fucks the youth out of me or out of any naive young boy. And beyond that, or beside it, in this emptiness where love for Andy finally merges with love for people who may not even exist, memory and recognition have become almost irrelevant . . . that 'almost' being all that remains between us: a word in the vortex, made with Promethean lips.

Love and faith are aspects of the same terrible experience. Andy has given me the terms of reference with which to recognise love. Siegfried, if nothing else, has shown me how to recognise lack of faith. And Janet? She reminds me to smile at it all occasionally – the tired, playful smile of one whose triumph hides itself in defeat. Her secret is an awareness that neither defeat nor victory exist, that torment and serenity are just two of the growing buds that await the sun with equal patience.

I struggle against thinking that any of these three is extraordinary. Such thoughts really do destroy all hope. But it's a constant battle. Somewhere – heart, head, bones? – I know that no-one else will ever so disrupt the essences of me as they have done. They have left me and the world endlessly changed, and so they are extraordinary for me, if only because they were the three who happened to meet in my deepest heart.

Now is a difficult moment. I am almost lost, despite my strength. If only you knew how fragile that strength is in comparison to Andy's – his ability to give without any expectations of getting *more* in return. Hope is different from expectation.

Now is a difficult moment, when God is just a shabby image of any ordinary person and the innocence of this First World is so long dead that it is no longer even rotting. It's a luxury still to feel pain after relieving the agony of an empty stomach, a luxury to try and sustain faith in this world which could so easily have been different, but which is just itself; a self that almost begs me to trample on it for what it is, but which instead I reluctantly adore. What then, if at this moment, love and faith are dreams like all the other great dreams? Perhaps there are only tactics, poems and listening, no dreams to come true.

The world is more fragmented than I, and I can no longer judge its value, I can only welcome it and all its mad Buddhas. I can only hover uncertainly in that fluttering of wings which insists on existing between faith and doubt.

I say these words uncertainly. I dare to say love. It's a word that keeps the muscles moving, the wings beating, whether mine or someone else's. I dare to hope, but only because I have no choice and because I have no control over it. I have only this one chance of hope.

There is neither courage nor fear in the uttering of a word like love. There is neither belief nor absence of belief in it. It is just a word to be kept for its own sake or to be discarded in desperation, like a memory.

At Greenwich, the sky is black and empty, in a solemn but undramatic mood. Who knows what colour the river is by now? Images expire in this sort of atmosphere, leaving only traces of graffiti along the walls of the tunnel by which we shall walk to the other side of the water. At the end of the tunnel we shall part silently like cats at dawn, not needing to show our inadequacies with mumbled words. We have survived and this is our ritual communion, a last kiss at first light.

new fiction titles published by GMP include:

Tom Wakefield
Drifters

ISBN 0 907040 49 7 (pbk)
50 0 (cased)

Following the success of his novel *Mates*, Tom Wakefield tells the stories of a group of gay men each in his own way isolated and adrift in a heterosexual world. 'Wakefield is an accomplished narrator, detached, witty and knowing . . . The stories are extremely moving' (*The Times*). 'Exudes a complexity and sincerity which mirror life and prove unforgettable . . . Read, digest and enjoy' (*Time Out*).

Simon Payne
The Beat

ISBN 0 907040 70 5 (pbk)

Friday night in a city park, and a young man is found battered to death in a public toilet. But this is no simple case of queerbashing. Six strangers hold the answer; they alone know what really happened that evening – when the intended victims suddenly struck back.

Graeme Woolaston
Stranger Than Love

ISBN 0 907040 81 0 (pbk)

Eddie's fascination with Rick, his young heterosexual neighbour, becomes an obsession which threatens to drag him ever deeper into self-doubt and uncertainty. But his discovery of the secret of Rick's past forces both to re-examine their deepest feelings and beliefs, as they find themselves developing a bond just as powerful, yet somehow stranger than love.

new titles in our art and photography series:

Philip Core
Paintings: 1975–1985

ISBN 0 907040 67 5 (cased)

In the ten years since his arrival in London, this young American painter has produced a large output of striking work which has understandably captured wide media attention. As this retrospective album demonstrates, Philip Core is essentially an artist dealing with serious themes in a contemporary idiom: 'an intellectual and witty painter working in a representational way' (*Max Wykes-Joyce*).

George Dureau
New Orleans

ISBN 0 907040 47 0 (pbk)
83 7 (cased)

An album of this celebrated photographer whose extraordinary portraits embrace both beauty and disfigurement. 'What makes Dureau's photographs truly remarkable is their capacity to see and record human dignity. (*Edward Lucie-Smith*).

Juan Davila
Hysterical Tears

ISBN 0 907040 87 X (cased)

The scandalous and acerbic paintings of this Chilean artist now resident in Australia make a provocative addition to our Art series.

Not for sale in Australia.

Wilhelm von Gloeden
Taormina

ISBN 0 907040 75 6 (pbk)

This portfolio of 20 nude studies is the first publication in Britain of this pioneer of plein air photography, showing his incessant fascination with the vestiges of pagan antiquity still so evident in the Mediterranean landscape and culture.

Not for sale in Continental Europe.

GMP also publish a wide variety of books in other areas, including biography, drama, health, history, humour and politics. Our full catalogue is available from GMP Publishers Ltd, P O Box 247, London N15 6RW. In North America, order from Alyson Publications Inc., 40 Plympton St, Boston, MA 02118.